Killing Time

M.C. Beaton
Killing Time

AN AGATHA RAISIN MYSTERY

WITH R.W. GREEN

MINOTAUR BOOKS
NEW YORK

First published in the United States by Minotaur Books, an imprint of St. Martin's Publishing Group

KILLING TIME. Copyright © 2024 by M. C. Beaton Ltd. All rights reserved. Printed in the United States of America. For information, address St. Martin's Publishing Group, 120 Broadway, New York, NY 10271.

www.minotaurbooks.com

M. C. BEATON® is a registered trademark of M. C. Beaton Limited.

Library of Congress Cataloging-in-Publication Data

Names: Beaton, M. C., author. | Green, R. W. (Novelist) author.
Title: Killing time / M.C. Beaton ; with R.W. Green.
Description: First U.S. Edition. | New York : Minotaur Books, 2024. | Series: Agatha Raisin Mysteries ; 35
Identifiers: LCCN 2024019596 | ISBN 9781250898708 (hardcover) | ISBN 9781250898715 (ebook)
Subjects: LCGFT: Detective and mystery fiction. | Novels.
Classification: LCC PR6052.E196 K55 2024 | DDC 823/.914—dc23/eng/20240426
LC record available at https://lccn.loc.gov/2024019596

Our books may be purchased in bulk for promotional, educational, or business use. Please contact your local bookseller or the Macmillan Corporate and Premium Sales Department at 1-800-221-7945, extension 5442, or by email at MacmillanSpecialMarkets@macmillan.com.

Originally published in the United Kingdom by Constable Books

First U.S. Edition 2024

10 9 8 7 6 5 4 3 2 1

For Mateu and Joana,
who always provide such a wonderful welcome at
Llenyater in Pollensa

Foreword

How many cameras can you count in your street, or in the area where you live? You can spot them on buildings, on masts, attached to streetlights, mounted on traffic lights or on the lights at pedestrian crossings. Maybe you can hazard a guess at how many there are near where you live, but what about across the whole country? In the UK, including the relatively new "doorbell cams" that have become ever more widespread over the past few years, there are around six million cameras keeping an eye on us. There are even more in the United States and plenty all over Europe, not to mention China.

For some people here in the UK, six million cameras is a disturbing figure, conjuring up old Orwellian paranoias that "Big Brother is watching you." The truth is that the vast majority of the footage captured on camera in the UK is never watched at all. Unless an incident has occurred that might warrant a householder, a business owner or a police officer trawling through hours of recordings, most camera footage is simply stored for a while and then deleted.

If officers can get their hands on them before they're wiped, video recordings can be incredibly useful to the police in establishing exactly what happened at a crime scene or tracking suspects and their vehicles. Police officers use camera images on a daily basis. Not everyone, however, is keen to share their video with the authorities and, in many cases, those running businesses with security cameras don't even know how to retrieve the footage. If you own a shoe shop, after all, you can be expected to know all about shoes, but maybe not so much about video technology. You can be fairly sure, therefore, that, most of the time, absolutely no brother, big or little, is watching you. On the other hand, if you were to get yourself caught up in any dodgy dealings in Carsely, Mircester or any other part of Agatha Raisin's stomping ground in the Cotswolds, you can bet your burglar's balaclava that Agatha will be watching.

For a private detective like Agatha, a strong grasp of how useful tech works is a necessity. When M. C. Beaton—Marion—first sat me down to talk to me about Agatha and the other characters in her books, she was able to describe Agatha's approach to gadgets in no uncertain terms, mainly because, as in so many things, Agatha's attitude was very similar to her own. She explained that Agatha might, at first, be suspicious of something new but, whether it be a new TV remote, a new phone, a new computer, a new iPad or a new camera, Agatha would doggedly stick at it until she had mastered the thing. She would never allow the youngsters on her staff to think that she couldn't keep up, even if it practically drove her doolally trying to do so.

Cameras, of course, in all their forms, are an essential tool of the investigator's trade. Agatha almost came a cropper once while up a ladder at a bedroom window trying to take a picture of a philandering husband with his mistress, so she's well aware of how vital photographic evidence can be. In *Killing Time*, it's fair to say, she and her team make good use of security cameras at home in Carsely, in Mircester and even in London, just as any investigator in the real world would want to do. Photographs and video images can provide cast-iron evidence and make or break an alibi, but, for Agatha, things that remain unseen on the video screen become paramount. Her understanding of the tech helps to keep her ahead of the game.

Real-world places often sneak into Agatha's world and that was always an entirely deliberate ploy on Marion's part. She was happy to send Agatha off to distant lands, generally to some of Marion's own favourite places—France, Cyprus, Turkey or even South America—but always stressed that Agatha had to come home to the Cotswolds because the area is one of the book's main characters, and the most important elements of the story should unfold there. Some rules, as Agatha points out towards the end of *Killing Time*, are there to be broken and Marion certainly wasn't averse to doing so. In this book Agatha's foreign jaunt gives her a major headache but also a little respite just when she looks like she might be overwhelmed by events. Where better to recharge your batteries than in the loveliest area of a beautiful Mediterranean island? Agatha ends up in Pollensa in Mallorca (yes, it *is* one of my favourite places) but, don't worry, she's back home in the thick of things before long.

The real world and real places may always have a part to play, but in *Killing Time*, Agatha also delves into a real-life mystery. The Campden Wonder is the story of the strange disappearance of William Harrison in 1660. For those of you who may be reading this before having read the book, I won't go into Harrison's tale here save to say that people have been puzzling over it for the best part of four centuries. The version outlined here is really just the bare bones of the story. If you want to find out more about it, the Campden & District Historical & Archaeological Society published a very informative booklet written by Jill Wilson, *Mr. Harrison Is Missing*, which is well worth a read. There are also masses about the whole mystery online, as you would expect. One thing I wasn't able to find was a theory anything like Agatha's, although that doesn't mean it's not already out there somewhere!

I hope you enjoy Agatha's latest adventure and meeting up with all our old Cotswold friends for another bout of murder and mayhem!

R.W. Green, 2024

Killing Time

Chapter One

"So this is where the murder was committed . . ." Agatha Raisin leaned against a wooden gate, craning her neck to peer into the meadow beyond. The shallow, grassy slope glistened with moisture, the morning sun having banished the overnight frost, leaving only furtive patches of white cowering in the sparse shade of leafless trees and the more substantial shadows lurking behind stone walls.

"It was around here that William Harrison's slashed hat and bloodstained scarf were found." Sir Charles Fraith stood behind her, leaning against his Range Rover, the large car dominating the roadside turn-off leading to the gate.

Agatha gave up straining to see into the meadow, instead stepping towards a stone stile set in the perimeter wall that gave access to a public footpath. She put one foot on the stile, then changed her mind. The four-inch heels on her mauve suede shoes were not designed for climbing over walls, even this low, waist-high boundary. Slipping off the shoes, she handed them to Charles.

"Here," she said. "Look after these. I want to take a look at the crime scene."

When she pushed herself up onto the stile step, she felt the unmistakable pop of a seam stitch at the back of her skirt. She sighed. The skirt had been a little tight when she first eased herself into it earlier that morning but it was the perfect purple to complement her new shoes. Surely it should have slackened off with wearing, not shrunk even tighter? She hitched it up, easing the strain but raising the hemline well above her knees. There was a murmur of approval from behind her. She turned and glowered at Charles.

"Well," he said, shrugging and smiling, "you've always had great legs."

"You'd best not try lines like that on any of your new employees, Charles," she warned him with a wag of her finger. "You'll be accused of using inappropriate language and sexism, and likely be sued for compensation for the distress you've caused."

"You needn't worry about that," Charles said, smiling. "I've brought in the very best people at the vineyard, in the winery and in the ice-cream business for that matter. I'm not going to risk losing any of them now that we're up and running. You can count on that, Aggie."

She gave him a cool look out of the corner of her eye. He'd used that name again. It was fine when they had been together, when they had been lovers, but once his dalliances with younger women had put an end to that, the pet name, "Aggie," had become an irritant. She had warned him countless times not to call her that, but old habits, especially in a man like Charles, who had never grown accustomed to letting anyone tell him what to do, died hard. In any case, she had a murder scene to scrutinise. She concentrated on traversing the stile without splitting any seams and took a couple of paces on the meadow's wet grass, ignoring the moisture seeping into the soles of her tights.

To her right she could see the graveyard of St. James' Church in Chipping Campden and the ornate church tower. In front of her, across the wide, grassy slope, lay fields and trees stretching off towards distant, hazy hills. The far edge of the meadow was marked by another stone wall and, dominating the wall, a curious, three-storey stone building with twin gables in its slate roof. Four pinnacles, like small minarets, rose from each corner of the building. Although poor imitations of their far more majestic counterparts proudly adorning the church tower, they still managed to lend the building an air of grandeur.

"What's that house over there?" Agatha asked, pointing towards the building with one hand while using the other to shield her eyes from the low winter sun.

"That's the East Banqueting House," Charles replied. "Looks rather splendid in this light, doesn't it?" He reached into the pocket of his heavy tweed shooting jacket, retrieving his phone to snap a picture of the scene. "It was once part of Campden House, although the old mansion was burned down in 1645."

Agatha turned to face him. She had seen no sign of any police tape, nor notices warning the public to stay clear, nor anything at all to indicate that a murder investigation was underway. She frowned at Charles, then instantly imagined her eyebrows, normally high, graceful, well-manicured arches, stooping to meet low on her forehead like two kissing snakes. She felt a wrinkle puckering. That would never do. She released the snakes.

"When exactly did this murder take place?" she asked.

"Ah, yes," Charles said, tucking his phone back into his pocket. "That's the really interesting bit. William Harrison went missing on the sixteenth of August 1660."

"The sixteenth of . . . ?" Agatha stomped back to the stile as well as anyone could stomp in stockinged feet on soggy grass, mounting the stile with scant regard to the danger of a split seam. "You told me there was a mysterious murder to be solved here, not some ancient fairy tale from nearly four hundred years ago! You've hoodwinked me into coming along this afternoon!"

She snatched her shoes from him, managing to fix him with a look of simmering fury while still accepting his arm for balance as she crammed her damp feet back into her shoes.

"I promised you a proposition that would interest you, a murder case that would fascinate you, and Sunday lunch," Charles said calmly, trying hard not to seem too amused by what he recognised as a relatively mild manifestation of the infamous Raisin temper. "We haven't even scratched the surface yet."

"Well, you can scratch it on the way to the restau-

4

rant," Agatha said, yanking open the car's passenger door. "Let's go!"

"First, the murder," Charles said, climbing into the driver's seat and starting the engine. "William Harrison was a well-respected man in this area. He was steward of the estate that belonged to Lady Juliana Noel, whose father built Campden House. Lady Juliana no longer lived in the area, but she trusted Harrison, who had worked for the family since her father's time, to run the estate. He set off to collect rents from Lady Juliana's tenants one afternoon, telling his wife he would be home in time for supper, but he never returned. She sent their servant, John Perry, out to look for her husband, but Perry didn't come back that night either."

"Was he killed, too?" Agatha slipped her shoes off again, letting the car's heater warm and dry her feet.

"No, he showed up the next morning when Harrison's nineteen-year-old son, Edward, went out looking for his father."

"Where was Harrison going?" Agatha asked, and Charles felt a flush of triumph. In that instant, with those two questions, he knew he'd piqued her interest and that now there would be no stopping her until she knew all the details.

"Actually, we're heading in that direction now," he explained. "Harrison aimed to collect rents from the villages of Charingworth and Paxford, and also call in at Ebrington on the way home. We're booked for lunch at the Ebrington Arms."

He pulled out onto the road, heading away from Chipping Campden.

"We'll be there in no time," he said. "It's only a couple of miles, a little less the way the old man would have walked across the fields."

"Old?" Agatha asked. "How old?"

"He was probably in his mid-sixties, but it was a journey he'd taken many times. He had worked for the Noel family pretty much all his life. He was also on the board of the local grammar school—a very methodical, particular and proud man by all accounts."

"He'd also have been very old for the time, wouldn't he? People didn't live so long back then."

"There's certainly some truth in that," Charles said, his head rocking from side to side as though weighing points for and against with his ears. "Infant mortality was dreadfully high but if you made it to adulthood and then into your twenties and were still reasonably healthy, you were clearly made of strong stuff. If you ate well and kept active, you could expect to live on into your seventies."

"So what did actually happen to him?"

"Therein lies the mystery!" Charles slapped a hand on the steering wheel to emphasise his point. "John Perry's account of how he went looking for his master didn't make much sense, so the local magistrate had him locked up to make sure he didn't disappear. Villagers were organised into search parties to try to find Harrison, but all they turned up was the hat and scarf."

"I assume the magistrate would then have suspected foul play."

"Quite right. John Perry was questioned again, and

this time he pointed the finger at his brother, Richard, and their mother, accusing them of having bumped off old Harrison to rob him of the rents he had collected. He said they told him they were going to dump the body in a pond or a cesspit."

"Yuck! Were the mother and brother still in the area?"

"Yes. They were arrested but denied everything. Look—we're almost there."

An attractive, modern-looking house faced with mellow Cotswold stone came into view on the left, and the ditches and hedgerows that had lined the road gave way to neatly trimmed grass verges. Charles followed the road round to the right where Ebrington's older cottages crowded in on both sides before they came upon a short yet elegant terrace of houses with expertly thatched roofs. Agatha made a mental note to make enquiries with the owners should she ever need work done on the thatch of her own cottage in Carsely.

Turning right onto a road signposted for Paxford and Blockley, the Ebrington Arms appeared ahead of them, the sign above its quaint bay window announcing it as a Licensed Victualler and Retailer of Spirituous Liquors. Agatha hoped they also served hearty meals as she hadn't eaten a thing since the lasagne ready meal she had nuked in the microwave the evening before. Her quiet, relaxing Saturday night in had almost been ruined when she'd attempted to watch some mindless garbage on TV, but she had rescued herself from the professionally feigned exuberance of a game-show host and the ecstatic howling of his studio audience simply by pressing the "off" button on her remote. She had then curled up on her sofa with her two cats, a glass of wine, and a much-thumbed copy of Agatha Christie's *Problem at Pollensa Bay* short-story collection.

Pollensa, on Mallorca, had a special relevance for her right now as the Spanish island was the next port of call for the *Ocean Palace Splendour* cruise liner. On board was John Glass, a former detective inspector with Mircester Police. The two had spent a great deal of time in each other's company since they had danced together at the wedding of their mutual friends, police officers Alice and Bill Wong. John was an expert dancer and Agatha had allowed him to sweep her off her feet during a subsequent series of dance dates. Their romance blossomed, their mutual love of dancing whisking them forward from dance partners to lovers. On retiring from the police, John had accepted a job as a dance instructor on the cruise liner but Agatha had refused to travel with him. Instead, they had agreed to meet in all the most romantic places visited by the ship on its voyage around the world. Their next rendezvous was to be in Mallorca.

Charles pulled into the car park at the side of the pub and they walked into the traditional country inn, its low ceilings supported by ancient oak beams. The bar was of gleaming, polished wood, proudly displaying pump handles labelled with a variety of real ales and, behind, shelves groaning under the weight of an impressive array of spirits. At one end of the room, beneath a massive timber mantelpiece, a log fire blazed in an age-blackened stove. Although it was distinctly chilly outside, the Ebrington Arms offered a cosy welcome, a little too warm for Agatha near the stove, so she was glad when the waitress who greeted them showed them to a table that wasn't too close to the fireplace.

"This looks like a lovely pub." Agatha's eyes roamed around the room, taking in her surroundings. "Would William Harrison have popped in here for an ale?"

"Probably not," Charles guessed. "I doubt he was the type to frequent drinking establishments and, in any case, this building was probably still a farmhouse back in 1660. It's someplace I don't believe we've ever tried before. Someplace new for us, in keeping with the new proposal I want to discuss with you."

"First things first," Agatha said, removing her wool jacket to hang it over the back of her chair. The lilac silk top was warm enough for sitting at the table. "You haven't finished your murder mystery story."

"Ah, yes," he said, clasping his hands together to help concentrate on gathering the threads of the tale. "Ponds and cesspits were drained and rivers dragged, but there was still no sign of a body. John Perry was questioned again and he further embellished his story. He now claimed that there had been a break-in at his master's house a few months before. It was a Sunday and Perry had been at church with the Harrison family. Servants were expected to accompany their employers to Sunday worship. They returned home to find they had been robbed. Around £140 was missing, a substantial sum back then, equivalent to many thousands of pounds today.

"Although he had said nothing at the time, Perry now maintained that the burglar had been his brother, Richard, who had forced him to say where money was kept in the house and to point out the best way to break in. He also claimed that Richard and their mother, Joan, had demanded he keep them informed of Harrison's movements, so they could plan an ambush in order to steal the rent money. He knew they were out to get Harrison that August evening and even caught them in the act. He said Harrison was laid out on the ground and Richard was on top of him, strangling him, while his mother counted the loot. He pleaded with them not to kill his master, but they told him to get lost."

"It sounds to me like Perry was what we might call a vulnerable person," Agatha said, sitting back in her chair, perusing the menu, yet still concentrating on what Charles had to tell her. "He was easily led and easily manipulated by his family. Sadly for him, he was still an accomplice."

"That's also how the judge at the September assizes in Gloucester saw it," Charles confirmed. "He decided to try all three for the robbery at the house, but wouldn't proceed with a murder trial at that time because no body had been found. I should think he was hoping either that Harrison would reappear, or his body would be discovered.

"Then, a strange thing happened. Even though they had always said that John Perry's accusations were totally untrue, when they were tried for robbery, his mother and brother pleaded guilty."

"Really?" Agatha's eyebrows soared high enough to achieve a personal best. "Why would they do that?"

"It's thought they were poorly advised that their quickest route to freedom would be to plead guilty and then be acquitted under the 1660 Indemnity and Oblivion Act."

"The what? Never heard of it."

"I'm not surprised. It's not something that crops up much in conversation, or even in court, nowadays. The law was repealed years ago." Charles smiled, then saw a fleeting look cross Agatha's face and immediately knew she was wondering whether he was pulling her leg. "It was a law enacted by Parliament under Charles II as a general pardon for crimes committed during the English Civil War and its aftermath. The aim was to stop acts of vengeance turning into vendettas that could relight old fires and start another war."

The waitress appeared and they ordered a bottle of primitivo. When it duly arrived, Charles insisted that Agatha taste the wine. She declared it delicious, and the waitress poured a glass for each of them and took their food order. Agatha went for the breaded whitebait as a starter followed by roast beef, traditional vegetables and Yorkshire pudding. She had been enviously eyeing other diners' generously loaded Sunday roast platefuls ever since they had arrived, hoping all the while that no one else could hear her stomach rumbling the way that she could. Charles opted for leek-and-potato soup and the roast beef.

"You've clearly been putting your history degree to good use on the Harrison case," Agatha said once the waitress had departed with their orders. "So were the Perrys pardoned?"

"Pardoned for the robbery, but not the murder. They were held in Gloucester Gaol until the next assizes in March 1661 when a different judge decided that, body

11

or no body, all three of the Perrys should stand trial for murder.

"Then, partly because they had pleaded guilty to the robbery, the judge and jury found it difficult to accept their 'not guilty' murder pleas."

"John Perry was found guilty, too?"

"Yes. His story kept changing. His account of what had happened on the night William Harrison disappeared never really added up. At one point, he even said he'd agreed with his mother and brother that they should rob the old man, but had then chickened out when it came to killing him. Then he tried to retract the accusations altogether, saying he'd gone temporarily insane. In the end, the only thing the jury believed was that the three of them had stolen William Harrison's rent collections and done away with the old boy."

"Were they then pardoned for the murder as well?"

"Unfortunately for them, the Indemnity and Oblivion rule didn't apply to murder. All three were hanged on Broadway Hill, where the Broadway Tower now stands."

"They were all hanged together?"

"The mother first," Charles said, sampling his wine. "Some believed Joan Perry was a witch and that if she were hanged first, it might release her sons from whatever spell she had cast over them and they would then confess and reveal where old Harrison's body was buried."

"A witch?" Agatha shook her head in disbelief. "Ridiculous! Did her sons confess?"

"No." Charles paused for a moment while Agatha received her fish and his soup was placed carefully on the table in front of him. "Richard went to his death protesting his innocence and John said nothing to support his brother."

"They sound like a very strange family."

"I'm sure they were. I'm also pretty sure their neighbours in the area wouldn't have had much time for them. They may well have been regarded as a bad bunch, and the break-in at Harrison's house could well have been their doing. It wasn't uncommon for women held in low esteem to be accused of being witches. Joan may have been a petty criminal but she wasn't a witch, and the Perrys were most certainly not murderers."

"What makes you say that?"

"Because a year or so later, in 1662, who should show up in Chipping Campden but William Harrison himself!"

"He wasn't dead at all!"

"Far from it. He explained his disappearance with some cock-and-bull story about having been abducted, spirited away on a ship and sold into slavery in Turkey. He said he escaped when the bloke who bought him died and he then made his way back to England. Clearly, given that the supposed murder victim was still alive, the Perrys had been executed by mistake."

"But that's awful!" Agatha gazed out the window with a faraway look in her eyes, as if in an effort to see all the way to Broadway Hill. "The poor souls may not have been model citizens, but they didn't deserve to die for a murder they didn't commit. Why on earth did John Perry accuse his mother and brother of a crime that simply didn't happen?"

"Nobody knows," Charles said with a shrug. "The

story became known as 'The Campden Wonder' and the whole thing remains a mystery to this day."

"It's certainly that . . . a real mystery . . . but it's not why you brought me here, is it?" Agatha said, pushing the events of 1660 to the back of her mind in order to concentrate on the "proposition" that Charles had promised. "I'm afraid my professional services as an investigator don't extend to solving four-hundred-year-old conundrums, so let's drag ourselves forward into the twenty-first century, shall we?"

She took a sip of wine, the notion occurring to her that, following accepted convention, she should probably be drinking white wine with the whitebait, but primitivo was one of her favourites and this was a particularly fine bottle. In any case, she had roast beef on order, so to hell with convention. She tucked into her whitebait.

"Well, the truth is I need your help," Charles said, sounding like he was laying his cards on the table, although Agatha knew he was bound to be holding something back. Charles wasn't one ever to tell the truth, the whole truth and nothing but the truth. "Thankfully, I'm not in need of a private detective, but I do need a public relations expert."

"I don't do that anymore," Agatha said bluntly.

"I realise that, of course," Charles said, then paused, spooning soup into his mouth. "The trouble is, I've met lots of these PR people and they've all been. . . ."

"Bright, smiley and enthusiastic but ultimately full of crap," Agatha cut in.

"Pretty much." Charles nodded, laughing. "I need someone I can trust to handle a job that has to be done to a fairly tight deadline, and you were the best in the business when you ran your own agency in London."

Agatha eyed Charles suspiciously while finishing off the last of her fish with the final smear of curried mayonnaise sauce.

"Not interested," she said. "Raisin Investigations keeps me busy enough and I have plenty going on in my life without diving back into the PR world."

"At least hear me out," Charles said, confident that he had her attention at least until she had polished off her roast beef, which the waitress who cleared their plates promised would be with them shortly. "I want to stage the biggest event our area has seen in years. I want people to be talking about it far and wide. There is so much going on in the Cotswolds right now. Our farm produce is second to none whether it be meat and dairy or fruit and vegetables. Local barley is used to make award-winning Cotswold malt whisky, first-class gin is distilled using Cotswold wheat and a locally produced Cotswold sauvignon blanc took top honours against international competition. I want our wine, Château Barfield, to be up there with the best as well."

"Surely you're not actually producing wine already?" Agatha was surprised. "I wouldn't have thought your vines were old enough."

"You're absolutely right," Charles confirmed. "We won't be producing wine from Barfield grapes for another three years, but the winery is in operation using local grapes from other growers in the vicinity. We're ready to launch Château Barfield in April and I want to do it with a huge event at Barfield House."

"April?" Agatha scoffed. "We're already at the end of February. The kind of people you would want to attend the launch will have diaries booked out well beyond May."

"I have a few names already on board. Benjy's an old school chum and he's pledged his support." Charles gave the waitress a smile of approval as she delivered their main course.

"Benjy?" Agatha gave him a quizzical look, searching her memory for the Benjy she recalled meeting once with Charles. "You mean Lord Benjamin Darkworth, head of the Manor Hotels group?"

"Yes, that's the chap," Charles replied, sliding his knife through a beautifully tender slice of roast beef. "Dickie and Hog want to get involved as well, so does old Binkie and . . ."

Agatha munched on a roast potato, studying Charles's face while he reeled off a list of aristocratic friends and acquaintances. His skin was smooth and almost wrinkle free, giving him the appearance of a man at least ten years younger. Or was he was so fired with enthusiasm for his new ventures that he had acquired a vibrant, youthful energy she hadn't seen in him in years? Whatever it was, she couldn't help feeling the new, supercharged Charles was markedly more attractive than the laidback Lothario she had once known.

". . . and, naturally, I would expect you to charge a substantial fee," Charles concluded. "Pulling this all together will take a huge effort and you must be suitably rewarded."

Agatha dabbed gravy from her lower lip with her

napkin, noticed a smear of lipstick on the white cloth but resisted the temptation to rush off and reapply.

"Who do you want at this shindig?"

"Local suppliers and customers," Charles said coolly, trying hard to suppress the growing glow of triumph he felt at hearing her begin to ask questions, "but we need wine buyers, restaurateurs, hotel owners, pub chains, supermarket buyers—everyone who can help put Château Barfield on the map. We have a few potential partners already, but we need more and I want to impress them. I want an event that will have them associate Château Barfield with quality and feeling good. Say you'll do it, Aggie. It will be so much fun working together. I want the whole thing to be fun, spectacular and enormously . . . glamorous."

Agatha sampled some broccoli, eyeing Charles across the table. She could give him a fun day that people would remember and make it stunningly spectacular. As for glamorous—well, that was practically her middle name. He was sitting bolt upright, not quite on the edge of his seat but close enough for her to know that he was desperate for her answer.

"I'll think about it," was all she said.

"We don't have much time, you know, Aggie, and . . ."

"I said," Agatha stated bluntly, cutting him off as efficiently as she sliced into her roast beef, "I'll think about it."

By the time Charles delivered Agatha back to her cottage in Lilac Lane, it was already growing dark, although it was not yet six o'clock in the evening. He had resisted pressing her any further for an answer about the launch event for fear of her simply saying "no." He could tell she was interested. He knew her well enough to be sure that he'd intrigued her with the prospect of staging a fantastically "glamorous" event. That was the word that had been the real bait, the word that had dangled a sparkle of temptation. Agatha could create an event dripping with glamour and would take great delight in doing so, but was she finding the thought of it as irresistible as he hoped? Only time would tell. He watched her hurrying up her garden path, waiting until she had unlocked her front door before he headed home to Barfield House. If he knew Agatha Raisin, and he prided himself on knowing her better than most, he'd have her answer before midday tomorrow.

Agatha stepped into her hallway and was immediately ambushed by her two cats, Boswell and Hodge, who wound themselves round her legs, purring as though they were powered by tiny cat engines. She promised to feed them, shooed them out from under her feet and made her way upstairs to her bedroom where she kicked off her shoes before easing herself out of the purple skirt. She was amazed that it had survived the mammoth Sunday lunch, given the way that stitch had popped on the stile, but she now needed something a good deal less constricting. Although she would never dream of wearing them outside her own four walls, she pulled on a baggy pair of sweatpants emblazoned with Mircester United

Football Club's crest. They had been acquired during a recent case and had gone on to become something of a guilty pleasure when she was lounging around at home.

Enjoying the freedom of loose-fitting polyester cotton, she skipped downstairs to the living room where she lit the log fire she had laid that morning. Her central heating was set to provide acceptable background heat but she loved the comforting warmth of the open fire. She then surrendered to the cats' demands, feeding them in the kitchen before returning to the living-room fire with her phone in one hand and a gin and tonic in the other.

Roy Silver was lolling on the couch in his Kensington apartment watching TV when his phone rang. He let out a long sigh, considered ignoring it, but ultimately picked it up on the fourth ring.

"Roy, it's me," was all the voice said but, of course, he recognised her instantly.

"Agatha, sweetie! How lovely to hear from you!"

"I'll get straight to the point, Roy—I need your help."

"Ooooh . . ." Roy was suddenly all ears. "What is it, darling—another juicy murder case?"

"No, Roy, something far more glamorous," Agatha said, deliberately using the word she knew Charles had used to try to snare her. "It's the PR opportunity of a lifetime and I want to bring you in on it."

"Oh . . ." Roy made no attempt to disguise the disappointment in his voice. "Well, the thing is, sweetie,

I'm absolutely rushed off my feet right now, working all hours, and—"

"Roy, that's rubbish and we both know it. You have a fantastic team working for you who do all the donkey work. My guess is that you left work early on Friday afternoon, drove up here to the Cotswolds and spent all day Saturday riding at Tamara Montgomery's stables, then sped back down to London for some party or other in a swish nightclub. You got up late this morning, had lunch at the Devonshire Arms and you're now lying on your sofa watching an old Doris Day movie on TV."

Roy reached for his remote control, pausing *Calamity Jane* in order not to miss one of his favourite scenes— when the reluctant drag artist singing "Hive Full of Honey" in the Deadwood saloon had his wig whipped off by the trombone.

"Have I really become so dreadfully predictable?" he said, sounding wounded.

"Not predictable," Agatha assured him, "but utterly reliable. That's why I need you with me on this job." She described how the launch of Château Barfield would be the biggest event in the Cotswolds for years and heard a whistle of approval from Roy when she rattled off the names of a few of Charles's aristocratic chums.

"People will be talking about the Great Barfield Extravaganza until we're both old and grey," she said.

"Oh, come now," Roy replied, laughing and running a hand through his hair. "You and I are both far too fabulous ever to grow old, darling, and as for grey . . . well, that's simply never going to happen!"

"Exactly!" Agatha agreed. "So people will never stop talking about it!"

"I have to admit that working with you again is very tempting—the dynamic duo reunited. You were the best in the business. There was never a dull moment working with Agatha Raisin!"

"So you'll do it?" Agatha knew she had won him over. "I'll need you up here in Mircester tomorrow to get started. You can stay in my spare room and you can have a desk at my office in town. You should be able to keep tabs on your business in London while we pull the extravaganza together."

"You're on," Roy confirmed. "You know, I think this is going to be rather fun."

They said their goodbyes and Roy restarted the movie, turning up the volume in order to hear it as he headed for his bedroom. He had masses of packing to do, but nothing was going to stop him duetting with Doris on "Secret Love."

Agatha pressed a speed-dial number on her phone and listened to the phone at the other end ring for what seemed like an eternity. Finally, someone picked up.

"Barfield House," announced the unmistakable, fruity baritone of Gustav, Charles's butler.

"Gustav, it's me," Agatha said. "Put me through to Charles, please."

"I'm afraid I cannot announce anyone simply as 'me,' so whom may I say is calling?"

"You know perfectly well who I am, Gustav, just put me through!" Agatha drummed the fingernails of her free hand on the arm of her sofa. Gustav was more to Charles than just a butler. He had worked for the Fraith family for as long as Charles could remember, and during the lean years when Charles had struggled to keep the estate going, Gustav had acted as servant, cook, housekeeper, driver, gardener, handyman and whatever else was required. His exact age and ancestry were something of a mystery, although Agatha had heard he was part Hungarian. The one thing that no one could dispute about him was his absolute loyalty to Charles. That had led Gustav and Agatha to become allies in the past, when Charles most needed their help, yet the butler's innate snobbery had always compelled him to look down on her. He had disapproved of her relationship with his master, mainly because he did not regard her as the right sort of woman to take on the role of consort to the lord of the manor. He did not believe she had the requisite breeding. She did not have the correct family background. In short, Gustav did not consider Agatha to be a lady. When she called Barfield House, therefore, he put her through the same rigmarole each time.

"By the coarseness of your tone I surmise that I have Mrs. Raisin on the line," Gustav conceded. "I shall enquire if Sir Charles is taking calls this . . ."

"Gustav!" Agatha heard Charles yelling from his desk in the library to where Gustav stood at the telephone table in the reception hall. "If that's Agatha, for goodness' sake put her through!"

"As you wish . . ." There was a click and Agatha knew she had been transferred to the phone on Charles's desk.

"You know, Charles, you really should try using your

mobile phone or at least install a direct line," she chided. "Gustav gets worse as time goes by."

"I know," Charles said, chuckling, "but he's very useful for screening calls. Now, do you have some good news for me?"

"That depends on a number of things. I want to bring in Roy Silver to work with me—you know Roy—and our fees will be expensive. In fact, in order to create an event on the scale you appear to want in the limited time available, the whole thing is going to cost a fortune."

"I expected it would," Charles said. "I'm sure we can raise some of the cash from sponsors but I know we'll still be taking a big hit. It will be worth it for the press and publicity. So—can I take it that you'll do it?"

"You can. Once Roy and I have made some plans, I'll get a contract to you."

"Excellent!" Charles made no attempt to disguise the delight in his voice. "That's the best news I've had all week!"

"One more thing," Agatha added, almost as an afterthought. "What happened after the Perrys were hanged? I mean, what happened to William Harrison?"

"Ah, 'The Campden Wonder'..." Charles replied, hoping Agatha couldn't sense the self-satisfied smile now spreading across his face. "Harrison carried on as before. There are even documents from the grammar school bearing his signature, so we know that his standing within the local community was unaffected. He went back to his normal, respectable life."

Charles's aged aunt, Mrs. Tassy, turned her head towards him as soon as the call ended. Tall and unbowed by her years, she moved towards a wing-backed leather armchair, having selected a book from the shelves that lined one wall of the room. As always, she was wearing a long, dark dress with a string of pearls at her neck almost as pale as her ghostly features.

"Why on earth are you bothering that Raisin woman with the old Chipping Campden story?" she warbled, her voice wavering but her diction precise.

"Because Agatha Raisin works best under pressure," Charles said, closing the folder on his desk, "and I now need her best work. Keeping her fully occupied will also make her happy and she'll be devoting a lot more time to me and Barfield. Hopefully, she'll come to associate being happy with being around me. In any case, we're going to be seeing a lot more of Aggie here at the house in the near future and that's just the way I want it. In fact, it makes me feel like celebrating—Gustav!"

The butler duly appeared, having paused outside the room long enough to allay any suspicion that he might have been listening at the open door, which, of course, he had been.

"Bring me some cognac, Gustav," Charles demanded. "I'm now in a rather good mood this evening."

"And a little more for me, I think," Mrs. Tassy said, tapping a bony finger on the empty brandy balloon on her side table. "It means I sleep well."

"You keep knocking it back the way you've been doing and it might mean you don't wake up," Gustav responded, collecting her glass.

"You know, Gustav," the old lady said slowly, treating him to a cold stare and a mirthless smile, "at one time in this house, impudence such as yours would have been rewarded with a sound thrashing. Fortunately, the Fraith family has always found your attitude endearingly amusing. Now run along and fetch the cognac, there's a good chap."

Charles crossed the room and settled himself on a sofa adjacent to his aunt's chair, stretching his legs out towards the log fire burning in the ornate marble fireplace.

"You need to be careful with Mrs. Raisin, Charles," the old lady advised. "She's not a woman to be trifled with."

"I'm not trifling with her," Charles said. "I'm giving her what she most needs. She's spent far too much time lately jetting off all over the world to meet up with that dancing ex-policeman of hers."

"I detect a note of jealousy," said Mrs. Tassy, staring at Charles over her reading glasses.

"Jealous? Me? Jealous of *him*?" Charles scoffed, then his features softened slightly. "Well, maybe I am a bit. I'm only human, after all. But now I can set her straight again. The old Aggie was never happier than when she had a mountain of work to get through and a horribly complicated crime to solve, and I've just given her both!"

Chapter Two

At the grandest, most fabulous party ever seen in the Cotswolds, Agatha was the centre of attention, surrounded by a crowd of handsome men and glamorous women, all stylishly dressed, sipping champagne and complimenting her on what a wonderful job she had done in staging the event, what a wonderful outfit she was wearing and how wonderfully slim she looked. Everything was wonderful. It was a word Agatha heard repeated over and over again, "Wonderful, wonderful, wonderful, darling!" Music was seeping through the waves of conversation from somewhere and the party atmosphere was positively tingling, yet, scanning all the happy faces gathered round her, Agatha was having trouble recognising any of them.

Then she spotted one man standing alone near a doorway. He was wearing a battered hat, a long black cloak, black knee breeches and grey stockings. She watched him looking furtively this way and that, uncomfortable and out of place. It seemed he knew he shouldn't be there and, when it slowly dawned on Agatha who he was, she could only agree—it was William Harrison! He looked straight at her, fear and panic in his eyes. She tried to push through the crowd towards him but a forest of partygoers' shoulders and elbows kept getting in her way. Harrison had spotted the exit and was hurrying to make his escape. She would never reach him before he got away! Then she then heard a noise loud enough to cut through the party chit-chat and background music—a regular, rasping, grunting noise that sounded for all the world like . . . snoring! That explained everything. It was a dream. She was asleep.

With the party swiftly dissolving around her, her eyes opened and focused on her bedroom, dimly lit only by the Lilac Lane streetlight filtering through the curtains. She glanced down at the foot of her bed where she could make out the shapes of Boswell and Hodge, sleeping peacefully. Neither of them was snoring. She tutted. Had she really woken herself up with her own snoring just when she'd had the chance to question William Harrison? *Don't be ridiculous*, she scolded herself. How could he tell her anything if he was only in her dream? He was simply part of her imagination. All he would have been able to say was whatever she imagined him saying.

She rolled over, half hoping that she might be able to slip back into the party dream. She recalled being able to do that once or twice in the past but, annoyingly, it wasn't something over which she had any real control. She tried silently repeating, "Wonderful-wonderful-wonderful," in her head until she fell asleep, soon drifting off to find herself not at the Cotswolds' most fabulous party of all time, but gliding across the ballroom floor on the *Ocean Palace Splendour* in the arms of John Glass. This wasn't the party. This was way better. This was a dream to stick with, and as her feet moved rhythmically in time to the music in her head, Boswell and Hodge abandoned the bottom of the bed for the safety of their basket in the corner of the room.

On the outskirts of Mircester town centre, just a few miles away from where Agatha was dreaming of a romantic interlude on a luxury cruise liner, the small, chic and exclusive jewellery store owned and run by designer Aurelia Barclay stood in silent darkness. Any passersby, and in this deepest, darkest pool of the night there were none, would have seen only an unlit shop with a desolate window display, the expensive, precious items that glistened there during daylight hours having been removed for secure overnight storage.

The flat above the shop showed no lights and the illumination on the elegantly lettered AURELIA DESIGNS shop sign was extinguished. The business, like all those around it, was locked down for the night.

Had anyone who chanced upon the shop looked closely, however, they might have seen a shadow flitting softly across the interior, and then, perhaps, another. With a little patience, anyone lingering outside might then have spotted the faintest glow of shielded torch-light. Despite the CLOSED sign on the door, Aurelia Designs had visitors.

Inside the shop, two black-clad figures crept into the jeweller's workshop, making straight for a tall steel safe that stood immovably fastened to both the wall and the concrete floor by hidden bolts. Making barely a sound, they knelt by the safe, examining its electronic keypad. Suddenly the room was a blaze of light and the two figures, their faces concealed behind black balaclavas, leaped to their feet.

"What the hell are you doing in here?" roared Aurelia Barclay, standing in the doorway that led to her flat upstairs. She was tall and slim with an unruly mane of red hair that tumbled down to the shoulders of her dressing gown.

The two intruders immediately dashed for the open back door but Aurelia bounded forward to cut off their escape, thumbing the mobile phone in her hand. In one fluid movement, the shorter of the two burglars swept a small hammer from the workbench, swinging it in Aurelia's direction. She raised an arm in an attempt to block the blow but the hammer slammed into the side of her face. Both raiders disappeared out the back door and Aurelia slumped to the floor. Her phone lay on the cold concrete by her head and, having already dialled 999, she heard the operator's voice asking, "Emergency—which service please?"

"Aurelia Designs," was all she could whisper before her eyes fluttered and closed.

The following morning, Agatha Raisin guided her car gently into her usual parking space in Mircester, the windscreen wipers working double time to clear the rain that was hammering down on the glass. Just as she switched off the engine, the rain turned to hail that drummed on the car's roof and bounced off its bonnet. This, she decided, was a squall she should wait out. Retrieving her handbag from the passenger seat, she rummaged for her lipstick then flipped down the car's sun visor to check her make-up in its mirror. No repairs were necessary but, she told herself, it was best to be prepared. A girl never knew who she might meet on her way to the office, even in filthy weather like this.

The hailstones continued to batter the car and Agatha watched them perform acrobatics on the bonnet. Not so long ago, she mused, she would have used the storm as an excuse to light up a cigarette. She was proud of the fact that she had given up, although she still found the smell of tobacco smoke so alluring that she could tell if someone was standing smoking on the pavement outside the King Charles pub in the lane opposite her office before she turned the corner from Mircester High Street.

The hailstorm passed as quickly as it had blown in, heading northeast to pummel the countryside all the way to Banbury. The rain then eased slightly as well and Agatha judged it safe to make a break for the office, pulling her collapsible umbrella from her bag. Stepping out of the car, she pressed a button on the umbrella handle to deploy the canopy. The spring-loaded red panels opened out, clicked into place, caught in the wind and shot off the end of their shaft, sailing towards entanglement in the barren branches of a tree fifteen yards away.

Agatha cursed and hurried round to the back of the car where she vaguely remembered that a proper, more robust, full-sized umbrella had been languishing in the boot for a few weeks. Opening the larger brolly into the wind, she sheltered beneath it, shaking water from her hair. She could feel her normally sleek, brown bob was in danger of being washed out of shape by its brief exposure to the rain. She sighed. Why was it when she'd spent so much time that morning to achieve the simple yet elegant style of classic Quant, she was probably going to arrive at her office looking like a jet-washed otter?

She hurried off along Mircester High Street.

The Raisin Investigations office was above an antiques shop in a winding, cobbled lane that led from the high street down towards Mircester Abbey. It was in the old part of the town centre where some of the buildings dated back more than three hundred years. Agatha far preferred this area of Mircester to the modern, drab concrete that dominated most of the rest of the town centre. She hated the soulless grey shopping precinct and municipal buildings that had been imposed upon the town in 1970s redevelopments, although she had nothing against modern design in principle. The latest clothes fashions, after all, were every bit as desirable as classics from the years gone by—well, some of them were. The wide-legged black trousers she was wearing were a bit of a blast from the past and were flapping like loose sails in the wind. She congratulated herself on not having chosen to wear the pleated skirt she'd been considering that morning. By now the skirt hem would have blown up into her armpits two or three times on the heavier gusts of wind. In any case, the trousers gave her the ideal opportunity to wear boots with precipitously high heels that were all but hidden, maintaining the secret of her overnight increase in height. She felt the wind tug at her umbrella and concentrated on keeping it under control.

As was so often the case, Agatha's first real problem of the day was how to cross the cobblestones of the old lane in order to reach her office. They were treacherously slippery when wet and there were heel-snapping cracks to negotiate. She crossed the cobbles on tiptoes, balancing like a tightrope walker with her bag in one hand and her umbrella in the other. Only when she reached the other side did she notice the large furniture truck parked outside Mr. Tinkler's antiques shop, completely blocking the door that led upstairs to Raisin Investigations. There was no one in the cab and when she ventured closer, carefully avoiding a spout of water cascading from a blocked gutter somewhere up on the roof of the building, she could see that the truck was parked too close to the wall for her to be able to squeeze through to her door.

Suddenly a gust of wind came howling down the lane, billowing into her umbrella and dragging it to arm's length before snapping it inside out. Agatha screeched in outrage, then gasped with shock as the cascade of water from the gutter was fanned directly onto her. Her hair was plastered to her head and icy rivulets ran down her neck.

"Snakes . . . and . . . bast . . ." was all she could whisper through the film of water streaming down her face. A moment later, a hand gently grasped her arm and she was led aside, out of the waterfall, out of the rain.

"Oh, dear, Mrs. Raisin," came a man's voice. "That was most unfortunate . . . most unfortunate. Please do come inside."

"Mr. . . . Tinkler," Agatha said, blinking water from her eyes. The antiques dealer was leading her into his shop. "Thank you."

"Oh, dear, dear me," said the portly shopkeeper, surveying her over his half-moon glasses with a look of grave concern in his misty green eyes. "I'm afraid this is all my fault, Mrs. Raisin. I am so very sorry. Please, you must stand here and warm yourself by the heater."

"What do you mean? How was this your fault?" She looked at him suspiciously, feeling the warmth from an electric fan heater permeate her damp trousers.

"The truck outside was delivering furniture to me." He indicated two comfortable-looking leather armchairs. "The driver and his mate must have popped round to the sandwich shop in the high street for some breakfast."

"Popped round to the . . . ?" Agatha gritted her teeth. "I've a good mind to pop round there myself and—" She caught sight of herself in an ornate wall mirror. Her hair was flat, making her ears stick out like jug handles, and the mascara that had promised to be "one hundred per cent waterproof" had lied. She had black streaks running down her cheeks and eyes like a post-punk panda. "On the other hand," she said quietly, "maybe not looking like this."

"I'm sure I have something in here that might help," said Mr. Tinkler, hurrying across the room to retrieve a large, plain cardboard box from the rear of his shop. It was the perfect accessory for his beige cardigan and baggy brown trousers. "Ah, yes!" he announced triumphantly after a short rummage, holding up an electric hair dryer. "It came in a batch of stuff from a house clearance, but I think it's almost new."

He placed the hair dryer on a side table and disappeared through an adjacent door, returning immediately with a clean, fluffy white towel.

"Take this," he said, "and use my bathroom to dry off. Let me take your raincoat. I'll hang it near the heater and, while you're sorting yourself out, allow me to make you a coffee . . ."

He waved a hand towards a shining machine made of copper and brass with a pressure gauge, various metal tubes and a large wooden-handled lever.

"The machine's not as old as it looks," he explained, "but I have a penchant for good Italian espresso."

Agatha took a quick look in the bathroom, which was small but neat and immaculately clean with a decent mirror above the hand basin. She had never taken time to get to know Mr. Tinkler, despite walking past his shop almost every day, and had always regarded him as a little odd, even slightly creepy. While it wasn't in her nature ever to admit that she might be wrong, her opinion of her downstairs neighbour was rapidly changing.

"In that case," she said, slipping off her coat, "I'd love to join you for a coffee, Mr. Tinkler."

Once she had restored her hair, her make-up and her dignity, Agatha settled into one of the leather armchairs opposite Mr. Tinkler, who handed her a plain white coffee cup on a matching saucer. She looked around the room. She had never been inside Mr. Tinkler's shop before, although she had glanced through the window many times in passing. The whole place was far more spacious than it looked from the outside and far less cluttered. There were many things displayed around the room but it was all actually quite neatly and logically laid out. There were brass coal scuttles and fire irons beside an ornate fire surround, crystal decanters and glasses sitting on a highly polished rosewood sideboard, Venetian glass ornaments in a display cabinet, leatherbound books in an oak bookcase, paintings, prints, ornaments, mirrors and even a suit of armour standing in a corner, clutching a wicked-looking battleaxe in its gauntlets. She took a sip and was very pleasantly surprised, declaring it to be the most delicious coffee she had ever tasted.

"And these chairs," she went on, "are actually very comfortable, aren't they?"

"They're Victorian," he said. "Finely crafted mahogany and leather in excellent condition. I have a client I know will want them, so I snapped them up when I saw them in the auction."

"You bought them at an auction?" Agatha said slowly,

an idea slowly forming in her head. "Do you go to many auctions?"

"Quite a few," he replied. "There are always some bargains to be had if you know what you're looking for."

"I have an event that I'm running in the not-too-distant future," she explained. "There will be lots of wealthy people there who have more money than they know what to do with. I think an auction in aid of charity might be rather fun, but I've never been to a real auction before."

"If you would like to see how an auction's run, I'm going to one this afternoon. There are a couple of things in the catalogue I'm interested in. Would you care to join me?"

"Mr. Tinkler, I think that's an excellent idea—I'd love to come along. It's a date!"

"A date? Really . . . I . . . dear me . . . all I meant was . . ." His cheeks flushed pink and he stared down into his coffee cup.

Agatha looked at him and smiled. Having met and spoken to him, she realised that he wasn't as old as he seemed, probably only in his early sixties, but he was clearly very shy.

"Don't worry, Mr. Tinkler, it's just an expression. It doesn't mean we're engaged or anything!" She laughed, trying to make light of the situation, but he was glowing ever more pink. She felt a twinge of exasperation at his timorous nature, then decided that it was endearing rather than annoying. He had, after all, been very kind about her drenching. She adopted what she hoped was a calm, reassuring tone. "I would be very grateful for your advice and guidance."

They agreed to meet in the shop later that day and, the furniture truck having gone, Agatha made her way upstairs to her office.

Her unscheduled coffee break with Mr. Tinkler meant that she was last into the office, her staff all settled at their desks by the time she strode in.

"Morning, boss!" Simon Black called, the young man looking up from the computer on his desk to give her his trademark wrinkled grin.

Agatha greeted him in kind, as she did with Patrick Mulligan, the sombre-looking former police officer, when he nodded a greeting. Helen Freedman, Agatha's secretary, bustled over to her as she crossed the floor to her private office, handing her three folders of paperwork for her attention—one with items to be signed, one with today's mail and the third with items that were least urgent. Toni Gilmour, Agatha's trusted deputy, then intercepted her before she could open her office door.

"You have an early visitor. I put him in your office and Helen brought him a cup of tea," she said, brushing a lock of blonde hair off her cheek. Her skin was smooth and flawless. Agatha was glad she had spent some time in Mr. Tinkler's bathroom reapplying her make-up. Toni wore very little make-up. She had no need of it. Youth and beauty walked hand in hand, but when youth fell behind, cosmetics were there to pick up the pace. In Agatha's opinion, knowing how to look good required a certain style, and that was something Toni had yet to acquire. She didn't like to admit to herself that she was jealous of Toni, yet, when she was being honest with herself, of course she was.

"Who is it?" Agatha asked.

"Mr. Mason from Mircester Chamber of Commerce," Toni said. "He wasn't supposed to be here until ten-thirty."

"Give me a couple of minutes to get settled," Agatha said quietly, "then come and join us, please, Toni."

Mr. Mason was a thin, small man wearing a dark grey suit and an unremarkable blue tie. Sitting in a chair in front of Agatha's oversized desk, he looked, she thought, too much like a mouse to be representing Mircester's business community, but he did have extraordinarily sharp, intelligent dark eyes. She bade him good morning, placed her phone and the folders on her desk, hung her coat on the stand in the corner of the room and dropped her handbag into a desk drawer while commenting on the foul weather and the leaking gutter. He said nothing. Not even a squeak.

"I wasn't expecting you quite so early, Mr. Mou . . . er . . . Mason," she said, thanking Helen for the coffee she delivered, as she did every morning. Mr. Mason declined a tea refill.

"I won't beat about the bush, Mrs. Raisin," Mr. Mason said twitchily. "I came early because the matter about which I have been instructed to talk to you has now become desperately urgent."

"Really?" said Agatha, sipping her coffee and immediately deciding that it wasn't a patch on Mr. Tinkler's. Toni then entered the room. "I believe you've met my colleague Miss Gilmour. She works with me on all our most important cases."

"Good, because the reason the chamber of commerce is seeking your assistance is of the utmost importance to the whole of Mircester," Mr. Mason assured them. "Our members include all of the most prominent business-people in the area. I assume you will have heard about the recent spate of burglaries at business premises?"

"I have," said Agatha. "The break-ins have been mentioned in the *Mircester Telegraph*."

"Indeed," Mr. Mason agreed, "but the latest burglary has yet to make the papers, and it is the most serious of all."

"What was taken?" Toni asked, poised with a notebook and pen.

"Nothing," replied Mr. Mason, "but one of the leading lights in the Mircester business community was brutally assaulted. Aurelia Barclay disturbed the thieves as they tried to open her safe and was bludgeoned as they made their escape. She is now in hospital."

"That's dreadful!" Agatha said. "I've met Aurelia. I even bought some earrings from her. She's an extremely talented designer. How badly was she hurt?"

"That I don't know," Mr. Mason said, "but the chamber decided at the end of last week, before this latest outrage, to ask you to step in. We would like you to catch whoever is responsible. As of this morning, we want you to do so before anyone else is injured . . . or worse."

"But the attack on Aurelia Barclay and the other robberies are surely matters for the police," Toni pointed out.

"I agree, Miss Gilmour," said Mr. Mason, nodding and becoming increasingly agitated, "but the police have completely failed to stop the crime wave and now, especially considering what happened to Miss Barclay, we need to find the perpetrators of these crimes and protect our businesses. The members of the chamber are more than willing to cover whatever fees you may charge, Mrs. Raisin. We must put an end to this outrage whatever it costs!"

"First things first, Mr. Mason," Agatha said, holding up a hand as if to stop the rampaging mouse in his tracks. "I want to find out how badly injured Aurelia is and if she's able to talk to us. That may give us a better idea of who we're dealing with. I need to consider the scale of the operation we would have to mount, and how it would affect our current caseload. Then, if I'm confident we can help, we may be able to come up with a plan and, if our proposals meet your approval, then we can discuss fees."

"I can't stress how urgent this is, Mrs. Raisin . . ."

"I understand, Mr. Mason. I will get back to you within twenty-four hours."

Agatha showed Mr. Mason out, promised again to be in touch the following morning, then addressed her staff in the main office.

"I'm postponing the usual Monday morning case catch-up," she said. "I need to get to the hospital to see Aurelia Barclay. Patrick, I want you to find out all you can about this morning's visitor, Mr. Mason, and who's involved at the chamber of commerce. Usual rules—I don't want us working for anyone until we're sure who they are.

"Simon, take a look at our current cases. See if there's

anything urgent needs doing today and let me know. Helen, Roy Silver will be arriving at some point this morning. Let him have the desk by the window. He'll be working on a special project with me. Toni . . ." Agatha glanced out the window to see the rain falling relentlessly and decided against a second drenching, ". . . hang on a second."

She popped into her office, fished her handbag out of its drawer and then stood in the doorway.

"Toni, you're with me. Bring my car round, would you?" She tossed her car keys to Toni. "I need to take a quick look at the paperwork on my desk."

Had Agatha not known she was walking along a corridor in Mircester General Hospital, had she suddenly been transported there with a wave of a magician's wand, she would have realised in an instant where she was. The diffused lighting that left barely a shadow anywhere yet rarely provided enough illumination either, coupled with the aroma of disinfectant and linoleum polish, created a uniquely flat atmosphere that was utterly unmistakable. It was vaguely depressing, as though it were a place that offered no hope, which, she considered, wasn't actually what you wanted from a hospital, was it? Maybe the place should be more jolly. Maybe it should make you smile. Still, clowns, jugglers, disco lights and dancing kittens wouldn't really be appropriate either, would they? Maybe the sombre, serious atmosphere was about right after all.

The nurse walking ahead of them, whose rubber-soled shoes squeaked on the linoleum every second step, showed Agatha and Toni into a small ward where there were just four beds. One was occupied by a very old woman who was fast asleep and so small that she made scarcely a lump in the bedsheets. In two others sat women who were only marginally younger and took an avid interest in the new visitors, studying them intently from behind glossy showbiz gossip mags. Agatha glowered at them and they both swiftly lowered their eyes back to their reading material.

Aurelia Barclay was sitting up in the fourth bed. Her jaw was supported by a wide dressing that ran up each side of her face then disappeared round the back of her head beneath her hair, turning it into even more of a fiery red mane than it was normally. The nurse drew a curtain around the bed to give them more privacy.

"Good morning, Miss Barclay," Agatha said, shaking her hand. "I'm Agatha Raisin and this is my associate, Toni Gilmour."

"Please, call me Aurelia," came the reply; Aurelia's lips were moving but her teeth remained clamped shut. "I remember chatting with you in my shop, Agatha. I never forget a customer, especially one who regularly appears in the *Mircester Telegraph* tracking down murderers. You bought the gold cascade earrings."

"I'm glad you remember me," Agatha said, "and thank you for agreeing to see us. Please don't try to say too much if it's causing you pain. I wanted to explain that we've been approached by the Mircester Chamber of Commerce . . ."

"I know," Aurelia interrupted her. "It was my idea to bring you in on this. I wish we'd done it sooner, then maybe those bastards in my workshop last night wouldn't have broken my jaw!"

"I take it the police haven't made much progress in tracking down the burglars?" Toni asked.

"None at all as far as I can tell," Aurelia said, then grunted, clearly experiencing a pang of pain. "Excuse me," she apologised. "I have to be careful how I speak. The police have told us they're doing their best, but they're understaffed and overstretched. I even heard one of the detectives—a tall, skinny idiot, seemed quite senior—describing the robberies as 'victimless crimes' because everything that was taken would be covered by our insurance."

"Ah, yes," Agatha said, nodding. "I think I know who you're talking about. There's no such thing as a victimless crime, and certainly not in your case. Can you tell me what the intruders looked like?"

"One was taller than the other but it was difficult to tell their actual heights," Aurelia explained. "They went from crouching by the safe to sprinting for the door, so they never really straightened up. Both were dressed all in black with black balaclavas. The shorter one hit me in the face with a hammer."

"A broken jaw is bad enough," Toni said, "but a hammer could have done even more damage."

"It was a small hammer—a planishing hammer for smoothing metal," Aurelia explained. "I use it a lot on my jewellery. It only weighs about five ounces."

"Nevertheless, it was a vicious attack," Agatha said. "I understand you lost consciousness, so it's remarkable that you can remember it all so well."

"Oh, I'll never forget those two scumbags," Aurelia said, stiffening with anger. "Some of last night is a bit woozy, but I can't get the image of that pair squatting by my safe out of my head."

"They weren't able to open it, were they?" Toni asked.

"No, but they looked like they knew what they were doing," answered Aurelia. "They didn't have time to get into the safe. I heard a noise and came straight downstairs. They'd already disabled my alarm system. They were real professionals."

Raised voices could suddenly be heard echoing along the hospital corridor and Agatha's heart sank when she immediately recognised one of them.

"Well, she'll see me!" bellowed a man's voice. "This is important police business. We are investigating an attempted murder!"

"I think we'd best go," Agatha said, standing to leave. "Thanks again for seeing us, Aurelia."

"You will take on the case, won't you, Agatha?" Aurelia pleaded. "I'd feel so much better knowing you were out there tracking them down."

"I'd like to," Agatha said, "but it depends on a number of other things. I'll be able to take stock of it all during the course of today."

Agatha and Toni pushed aside the curtain to be confronted by a tall, gangly man wearing a limp brown suit that hung on his bony frame like cast-offs on a scarecrow— Detective Chief Inspector Wilkes. He was accompanied by Agatha's friend, Detective Sergeant Bill Wong.

"What's this interfering woman doing here, Wong?" Wilkes barked, glaring at Agatha.

"I'm doing my job," Agatha said, fixing him with her bear-like eyes. "You should try that sometime."

"Don't try to bait me, Mrs. Raisin. I'm not interested in any of your drivel," Wilkes snorted. "Out of my way. This is official police business, not the lost cats and seedy snooping that fill your days. This is a serious crime."

"It's a shame Miss Barclay had to get hurt before you started to take things seriously."

"I don't need any lectures from a rank amateur like you. I think you'd best step aside."

"You think? I wondered what the burning smell was. Your brain cell's overheating again, isn't it?"

"Now you listen to me, you irritating upstart! If you get in the way of me investigating an attempted murder . . ."

"You're joking, right?" Agatha's head tilted slightly to the right. "This was a horrible incident, but you're wasting your time trying to make a charge of attempted murder stick. You'll never be able to prove the burglar used that hammer with intent to kill. The most you'll likely get is aggravated burglary and, knowing you, you'll probably bugger that up anyway!"

"Sergeant Wong!" roared Wilkes. "If this woman says another word, you are to arrest her for obstructing a police officer in the execution of his duty!"

"The only obstruction here is between your ears and . . ." Agatha paused as Bill stepped forward, giving her a look she knew meant she should bite her lip. On balance, she considered she had too much else she wanted to do that day than to give Wilkes the pleasure of leaving her twiddling her thumbs for hours at

Mircester Police Station. She allowed Bill to lead her off to one side while Wilkes marched into the ward, demanding to know which of the two women peeking out from behind their magazines was Aurelia Barclay.

"Don't push him, Agatha," Bill said softly, once they were out of Wilkes's earshot. "He can make life very difficult for you."

"Well, he's had plenty of practice at that," Agatha said, sighing. "How can you stand working for him?"

"In the police service we don't get to choose our bosses," Bill said, smiling. "Miss Barclay's been asleep, so we haven't had a chance to talk to her properly yet. I take it she's in there?" he added, pointing towards the curtained bed. Agatha nodded.

"She's wide awake now, Bill, and very angry," Agatha advised. "She'll have heard Wilkes out here and she'll be ready for him. I don't think she'll be as gentle with him as I was."

"I'll make sure she doesn't clobber him," Bill said, laughing, before stepping through the curtains just ahead of Wilkes.

"Aurelia seemed like a really nice woman," said Toni, "but we can't really help her, can we? Wilkes will throw the book at you if he thinks you're trampling all over his investigation."

"We've also got so much on at the moment that I think committing to tracking down burglars is a bit crazy," Agatha replied, "but, after that little run-in with Wilkes, well . . . life would be pretty dull if we didn't go a bit crazy now and again, wouldn't it? We'll nail those rats who battered Aurelia and to hell with Wilkes!"

Chapter Three

The rain had all but stopped by the time Agatha and Toni returned to Raisin Investigations, but winter was still making its presence felt in the chill carried by the wind. As soon as they were back in the warmth of the office, Agatha called a meeting and everyone filed into her room, carrying notepads and dragging chairs.

"Roy will be sitting in on our meetings for the foreseeable future," Agatha explained as Roy joined the group. "I'll explain why shortly. First, let's run through the most pressing work we have on at the moment. Toni?"

"The legal firm, Collins and Strauss, want us to track down a couple of witnesses for a civil case," Toni said, consulting the notes on her pad. "We have the Parkers' divorce case, legal papers arriving today that need to be served on behalf of a couple of solicitors and various employee background checks to carry out."

"Okay," Agatha said, settling back in her chair. There had been no surprises. The details of the ongoing cases were all safely stored in her memory. "I'll have a word with David Collins. That case won't be going to court for months, so I'm sure he can give us some more time. Simon, you can try tailing Mrs. Parker today. I doubt she'll be having her usual tennis lesson, but we need to know if she meets up with her handsome coach for a spot of indoor sport. Toni, you can press on with the background checks, and Patrick, you be ready for those legal papers. While you're waiting, find out all you can about the businesses that have been burgled—who they are, how long they've been operating, what was stolen and, most importantly, other businesses that might be targeted."

"So we're definitely taking on the case for the chamber of commerce?" Toni asked.

"We are," Agatha confirmed. "Once we've worked out a few more details, I will talk to Mr. Mouse."

"You mean Mr. Mason," Toni corrected her.

"That's what I said."

"No, you didn't. You said Mr. Mouse."

"Oh, don't be ridiculous, Toni."

Agatha turned towards Patrick, Simon grinned at Toni and Toni rolled her eyes before concentrating on her notepad.

"Patrick, do you think you can find a couple of your retired colleagues we could employ on night patrols of potential targets?" Agatha asked.

"Can do," Patrick said.

"Er . . . if there's overtime involved, boss, I'm up for

a few night patrols," Simon said with undisguised enthusiasm.

"Not on your own, Simon," Agatha said. "We'll do that in pairs. Toni? Patrick? Would you be up for a nightshift a couple of times a week?"

Both nodded.

"Very well, once we have your friends on board, Patrick, we can draw up a nightshift rota," Agatha said. "I'll talk to Mr. Mou . . . Mason later today. Toni, you and I can then interview each of the business owners who've been hit by the burglars."

"Er . . . weren't you supposed to be taking a few days off at the end of this week?" Toni asked Agatha.

"Yes . . ." Agatha paused, her mind drifting to John aboard the *Ocean Palace Splendour*, due to dock in Palma, Mallorca, in a few days, where the Mediterranean sunshine would be warming the island to a temperature equivalent to a pleasant, late spring day in England. "I may have to cancel that little break. In the meantime, I have some more exciting news. Roy is here to help me with plans for the biggest party the Cotswolds has ever seen!"

Agatha's announcement was met with raised eyebrows and murmurs of interest from around the table, along with a huge, beaming smile from Roy.

"We're staging a massive event to launch Sir Charles Fraith's new wine business," he explained, "and it's going to be sensational beyond words, my darlings. I've already got a whole list of ideas for the day and masses of contributors who want to be involved, from hot-air balloonists and showjumpers to exotic car clubs and top fashion designers who want to put on a show. It is going to be totally FAB-U-LOUS!"

"This is going to take up a lot of my time over the next few weeks," Agatha said. "It's not detective work, but I may have to call on your help from time to time. We're going to be very busy over the next couple of months, but the Great Barfield Extravaganza should be a lot of fun, too."

"If you need any help looking after the fashion models, boss," Simon said, holding his arms out to offer himself, "I'm your man."

"Thank you, Simon," Agatha said, shaking her head and ignoring the laughter from Toni and Patrick. "That might seem a little like throwing the cat among the pigeons, although in this case I think the pigeons would probably fling you right back again. We're also going to stage a charity auction," she added, checking her watch. "Roy, I'll ask Helen to grab us a sandwich for lunch, then you and I need to meet Mr. Tinkler downstairs to find out how an auction works."

Roy Silver talked almost nonstop about plans for the extravaganza from the time Agatha drove out of her parking space to the moment they reached the auction house, which turned out to be a converted barn on a farm a few miles outside Mircester, just off the road to Evesham. Mr. Tinkler sat in the back, saying nothing at all until they were about to leave the car.

"I do hope you won't be disappointed, Mrs. Raisin," he said, sounding vaguely apologetic. "This isn't a very glamorous place, but it really is a very good auction house."

Agatha looked up at the sign above the entrance where the words RANDALL AUCTIONS stood proudly in gold on a black background.

"I'm not sure what I was expecting, Mr. Tinkler," she said, "but I'm looking forward to the auction."

"You must be careful not to blink, cough or wave a hankie at the wrong time," Roy warned her. "Otherwise, you might end up paying a fortune for something you didn't even want."

"Actually, that's something of an old wives' tale, Mr. Silver," Mr. Tinkler corrected him. "I have registered as a buyer, and when we go in, I will be given a paddle with a number on it. I'll hold that up if I want to make a bid. You really can't bid on things by accident."

When they made their way inside and Mr. Tinkler checked in at the desk, Agatha was surprised at the number of people in the barn. There were dozens on seats arranged in rows, as though the occupants were attending a lecture or a school play, while even more people were standing around the perimeter where various items of furniture, large and small, were on display. The room was well lit and remarkably warm given how chilly it was outside. They picked a spot to stand on one side, where they had a good view of the proceedings.

"They were doing furniture this morning," Mr. Tinkler explained. "We'll be seeing smaller items this afternoon. I have my eye on some porcelain that I saw in the online catalogue."

The auctioneer took his place behind a lectern on a

small platform, introducing himself as Martin Randall. He was a tall, dark-haired, elegant man with the kind of winter tan that comes from an expensive Caribbean holiday rather than a sunbed or a bottle. He wore a well-cut suit with an expensive shirt but no tie. The auction premises might not, as Mr. Tinkler put it, be "very glamorous," but the auctioneer certainly was. Roy looked at Agatha then raised an eyebrow, cocking his head in Randall's direction, clearly expressing his approval.

"Steady, there, tiger," she chided him. "Waggling your eyebrows like that might buy you something you didn't mean to bid on."

"Not without the paddle, dear, remember?" Roy said, laughing. "He's a bit of a looker, though, isn't he?"

Agatha chose to ignore Roy, but was glad that she had taken the opportunity to touch up her make-up before leaving the car. Martin Randall was the sort of man she would not want to meet unless she was looking her best.

"We're starting the afternoon session," Randall announced, "as per the catalogue, with various ornamental figurines, vases and glass."

He went on to describe each lot as it was displayed by one of his team of assistants, who brought the items up onto the podium. He then scanned the room, taking bids and constantly gauging the level of interest. Telephone bidders were accommodated by one of Randall's staff using a couple of phones and another relaying online bids from a laptop. When he decided bidding on an item had gone as far as it would, Randall struck a small wooden block on his lectern with a gavel that he held, almost invisibly, in his hand. Agatha scolded herself for feeling slightly vexed that he wasn't swinging a wooden mallet at the block, as she had imagined he might. There was no point in feeling short-changed every time tiny details of real life failed to live up to your expectations. That could lead to an eternity of disappointment. She concentrated on keeping up with the pace at which bids were made, which could sometimes happen in the blink of an eye. Mr. Tinkler raised his paddle a few times on some chinaware, but didn't stay in the bidding to the end on anything.

"The thing is, Mrs. Raisin," he told her quietly, "you should know what you are bidding for, understand its value, and only bid as much as you believe it's worth to you."

Once the final piece of glass had been sold, one of Randall's assistants brought out a large, elaborate ornament that turned out to be a clock. It was golden with a round, white face, and above the face were the figures of a man and woman in Victorian garb, holding each other in a dance pose that was both gently formal and unashamedly romantic. Enamelled panels either side of the clockface showed images of other dancers. On a panel below the face were what looked to Agatha like a series of flower images.

"Oh, my," said Roy, admiring the clock. "That's quite something, isn't it? Wouldn't that look divine on your mantelpiece, Agatha?"

"Now you mention it," Agatha said, nodding, "yes, it would. And just look at that dancing couple . . . Mr. Tinkler, am I allowed to use your paddle to bid?"

"Yes, of course," Mr. Tinkler replied, passing the paddle to her.

"This is a rather charming nineteenth-century ormolu clock—that's gilded bronze—with delightful enamel inlays and a beautifully sculpted lady and gentleman dancing," Randall explained. "It is believed to have been made in Paris for a Russian gentleman, then found its way to Brussels before being inherited by the vendor, who's had it tucked away in an attic for decades. I should stress that the clock is not currently functioning, although the mechanism appears to be intact as far as we can tell, so there's no reason to believe it couldn't be repaired. In consideration of its condition, we'll start the bidding at one hundred pounds . . ."

Agatha shot her paddle into the air.

"An energetic one hundred from the lady on my left," Randall said, smiling at Agatha, then spotting a rival bid at the very back of the room. "One ten at the back there . . ."

"One-thirty!" Agatha called, waving the paddle.

Randall nodded to Agatha, then looked to the room, saying, "Another twenty?"

A paddle flashed on the far side of the room, then another in the middle.

"Two hundred!" Agatha yelled, holding the paddle above her head.

"Really, Mrs. Raisin," Mr. Tinkler cautioned her. "You mustn't bid more than it's worth. It's not even working."

"Yes, yes, I know . . ." Agatha glanced at him briefly, concentrating instead on the other bidders, who were all still in the game. The one in the middle of the room was a slim, pale man with thinning red hair. She couldn't quite see who was bidding at the back, but seated on the opposite side of the room was a woman with shoulder-length blonde hair. She was wearing a black coat, a wide-brimmed black hat and dark glasses. *That*, Agatha thought, *looks almost like a disguise, as if she doesn't want to be recognised, yet who wears a hat like that and sunglasses indoors unless they want to attract attention? Some sort of celebrity, perhaps?* It was hard to tell who she might be, but she was most definitely a rival. Agatha raised her paddle.

"Two thirty from the lady on my right," said Randall, then acknowledged bids from the middle and the back of the room. "Two sixty, two ninety . . ."

The woman in the glasses raised her paddle and four fingers.

"Four hundred?" Randall asked, pointing his gavel hand at her. She nodded. The balding ginger man flashed his paddle and mouthed something. "Four fifty from the gentleman in the centre," Randall continued, "Five hundred at the back, five fifty on my right . . ."

Agatha shot an agitated glower at the woman in black, who ignored her, staring straight ahead at Randall, who looked towards Agatha. She raised her paddle. She watched Randall look to the back of the room but the bidder there seemed to have dropped out. The ginger-haired man and the woman in black, however, were still in the game. Agatha stayed with the bidding through six fifty, seven hundred and seven fifty, at which point the ginger-haired man gave Randall a slight shake of his head.

"Ha!" Agatha whispered to no one in particular. "He's out. Now it's just me and her!"

The other woman raised her paddle for a bid of eight hundred pounds and Randall turned to Agatha.

"One thousand pounds!" Agatha shouted, eliciting a brief chorus of "Oooooh" from the room.

"Agatha, are you sure you—" Roy began, a note of nervous excitement in his voice.

"That bloody woman is not getting my clock!" Agatha snapped, stamping her foot as her rival raised the bidding to £1,100.

"Twelve hundred, thirteen . . ." Randall announced, and Agatha hissed with frustration.

"Two thousand pounds!" she roared, and a rumble of astonishment rolled around the room.

The woman in black turned her head slowly towards Agatha, examining her from behind large, anonymous, dark lenses. She then got to her feet and strode swiftly towards the exit.

"Are we all done at two thousand pounds? Selling at two thousand . . ." Randall banged his gavel on the block and Agatha gave a squeal of delight.

"I did it!" she said, bouncing on her toes, beaming at Roy and Mr. Tinkler. "I got it!"

Roy congratulated her with a loud whoop and a big hug.

"Normally it's all a bit dull here," Mr. Tinkler said, chuckling and patting his chest, "but you certainly livened things up today, Mrs. Raisin. Doesn't do my poor heart any good, though!"

In the cashier's office, Agatha settled the bill with her

credit card and was watching the clock being carefully cocooned in bubble wrap when Martin Randall appeared, introducing himself and explaining that there was a slight break in proceedings.

"That was a fiery little bidding war we had out there," he said, laughing. "It's a lovely clock, but I didn't expect there would be quite so much interest in it. The seller will be very pleased."

Agatha looked him straight in the eye, glad she was wearing heels that allowed her to do so. He had faint laughter lines around his eyes and smile wrinkles at the corners of his mouth, which gave him the air of a man who was relaxed and happy. Flashes of grey in his hair gave him a look of distinction but it was difficult to tell his age. She judged him to be anywhere between forty and fifty-five.

"As am I," Agatha said. "I wanted the clock from the moment I first saw it, and I'm a woman who always gets what she wants."

She felt a heavy bell of embarrassment clang in the pit of her stomach. Had she really just said that? "I'm a woman who always gets what she wants"? It sounded so arrogant and so . . . well . . . obnoxious!

"I've no doubt you are," Randall said, with a warm smile. "Might what you want include dinner sometime?"

"Yes, I think it might," she said, recovering her composure, her mind immediately turning to the extravaganza auction. "In fact, I think that's a very good idea. I'd love to talk auctions with you."

She gave him her card and he promised to call, then she hurried outside to meet Roy and Mr. Tinkler. She turned briefly, flashed Randall her best, most dazzling smile and gave him a cute little wave, which she immediately regretted. Why the silly wave? It was almost as mortifying as the "always gets what she wants" line. Why was she making such a fool of herself over this complete stranger?

"You fancy him, don't you?" Roy said, hitting the nail on the head and accepting the boxed clock while Agatha searched for her car keys.

"Nonsense," she said. "It's just that he may be useful to us with the charity auction, that's all."

Even as the words left her lips, she knew that was undoubtedly one of the least convincing lies she had ever told.

Roy sat with the clock in his lap all the way back to Mircester, then carried it to Mr. Tinkler's shop.

"Would you both like to come in?" asked Mr. Tinkler, unlocking the shop door. "I would love to take another look at your clock, Mrs. Raisin."

"Of course," Agatha said. "I'm sure we can spare a few minutes, can't we, Roy?"

Agatha and Roy sat on the leather armchairs, which were now behind an ornate screen, shielding them from the front of the shop, out of sight of passersby. The chairs were arranged in front of a table that Mr. Tinkler used as a desk. He served tea in delicate china cups, sat at the desk and asked Agatha's permission to unwrap the clock. It looked larger on his desk than it had at the auction room and Agatha had an uncertain moment when she wondered whether it would actually fit on her cottage mantelpiece. She said nothing, assured herself that it would and listened to Mr. Tinkler.

"It's a very fine piece," he said, studying the clock through his half-round glasses. "Rather unusual. Look, there are three winding arbors."

He pointed to three holes in the clockface, one by the three, one by the six and one by the nine.

"How many should there be?" Agatha asked.

"I'd normally expect to see one, or possibly two," Mr. Tinkler explained. "One would be for winding the clock mechanism and the second would be if there was a special chime, but I've no idea what the third might be for. It's such a pity it's not working."

"Can you fix it?" asked Agatha.

"Dear me, no, Mrs. Raisin, not me," he said, backing away from the clock slightly. "I really know very little about clocks. My brother, on the other hand, is something of an expert."

"I'd be happy to pay him if he can repair it," Agatha said.

"Oh, you must, Agatha," Roy said, running his hand over the dancing couple. "Hearing it tick would make it almost as if they were dancing in time."

"If you can leave it with me," said Mr. Tinkler, "I'll have him take a look at it as soon as possible."

They chatted for a short while, Roy once again enthusing about the extravaganza, finished their tea and prepared to leave. Mr. Tinkler showed them to the door, then paused.

"Mrs. Raisin," he said hesitantly. "Until my brother

comes to pick it up, would you mind if I displayed the clock in my shop window? It's such a wonderful object, I would love to put it on show."

"I think that would be absolutely fine, Mr. Tinkler," Agatha said, "as long as you don't sell it."

"Oh . . . dear me, no . . . I would never . . ." He stumbled over his words, utterly flustered, then caught the look in Agatha's eye. "Ah . . . that was one of your little jokes, wasn't it?"

"Thank you so much for taking us to the auction, Mr. Tinkler," Agatha said. She smiled, reached over and kissed him on the cheek. He flushed bright pink, then scurried off back into the shop to hide his bashfulness.

"Wait, look!" he called, carefully picking up the clock. "I'll show you where it can go."

He removed an art deco figurine of a ballet dancer from the shop window, gently settling the clock on the velvet-covered display stand in its place. Agatha and Roy watched the operation from the street, applauded Mr. Tinkler's positioning of the clock, then hurried upstairs as a light drizzle heralded the return of the rain.

No sooner had Agatha walked into the office than Helen Freedman handed her a small, square envelope with "AGATHA RAISIN" neatly handwritten in capital letters on the outside.

"The doorbell rang earlier and this was posted through the letterbox," Helen explained. "It's clearly been hand delivered. There's no stamp and no address."

"Thank you, Helen," Agatha said, frowning at the

envelope. Once she was back at her desk, she opened the mystery letter to find just one sheet of paper inside. Handwritten in the same, precise capitals used on the envelope were a few short lines:

<u>YOUR FINAL CASE</u>

FIND ME FIRST IN DOORS—SEE ME WEEP FOR A SECOND?

I AM IN ANSWER BUT NOT IF YOU BECKONED

THE END OF THE CUT IS THE FOURTH SIGN

AND THE FINISH ENDS AS YOUR BREATH, NOT MINE

Agatha stared at the note. What did it mean? What the hell was it? Some kind of prank, perhaps? She turned the paper over but there was no clue to identify from where it had come. She set the note aside when Patrick popped his head round the door. She asked him to take a seat but couldn't help glancing down at the bizarre note.

"Something bugging you there?" Patrick asked, indicating the note.

"No, well, yes, kind of," Agatha said, frowning. "Just

a weird note. Someone's idea of a joke, I should think. What have you got for me, Patrick?"

"Well," Patrick said, opening a folder he had brought with him. "Your Mr. Mason from the chamber of commerce seems like a fine, upstanding citizen. He's an accountant and handles everything from doing the books for small businesses to individual tax returns. He's a well-respected man who lives a quiet life, married with one daughter."

"He's everything I expected him to be," Agatha said, nodding. "Who else is involved in the chamber of commerce?"

"Lots of businesspeople from around the area," Patrick said, and ran through a list of some of them. "Most of these people are involved because being a member brings them business contacts and, as a group, they have more clout when it comes to dealing with the local authority on planning issues and suchlike. The chamber also gets involved in various charity things."

"Okay," Agatha said, browsing the list of business owners Patrick had passed to her. "Which of the businesses have been targeted in the burglaries?"

"They're the ones highlighted," Patrick explained, pointing to the lines marked in yellow. "They're all shops, obviously, and they all sell expensive items that are easy to transport and easy to sell on—electronics, watches, jewellery and the like. Nine of them have been hit in the last three months."

"Were they all the same as Aurelia's break-in? Alarm disabled, professional job?"

"They were," Patrick said, "and according to a mate

of mine who's still a cop, they all had one thing in common." He slid a printout of an online advertisement across the desk. "They all had alarm systems installed by this outfit."

"Sculley Security Systems," Agatha read from the printout. "Do you know anything about them?"

"Only that Stuart Sculley is a member of the chamber of commerce," Patrick said. "He has an office on the industrial estate at the old railway marshalling yards. I can keep digging on him if you want me to."

"Yes, please, Patrick. I think I may need to pay him a visit."

Patrick returned to his desk and Toni appeared moments later.

"Bill Wong's here to see you," she announced and Agatha asked her to show him straight in. Agatha walked round her desk to greet Bill with a warm hug.

"This is a surprise," she said, taking her seat and waving him into the one Patrick had just vacated. "It's not often we have an actual, serving police detective here at Raisin Investigations."

"Fortunately for you, as a law-abiding citizen, the police seldom have any reason to be here!" Bill laughed.

"How is Alice?" Agatha asked. She was almost as fond of Alice as she was Bill and had been instrumental in resolving an issue with Bill's parents that had almost scuppered Bill and Alice's wedding plans.

"She's just swell," Bill said, arcing a hand out from his stomach. "I think that's what people say, isn't it? She's doing really well and she's now starting to grow a real baby belly."

"That must be awful!" Agatha said, aghast at the thought of her midriff expanding beyond her control. "I mean . . . how is she coping with that?"

"She's loving it. She's not loving being stuck in the office, though. She much prefers getting out to crime scenes, but we can't have her taking on those sorts of duties right now."

"It must make things difficult, you both being police officers."

"We're coping, but I didn't really come here to talk about Alice and me."

"Let me guess," Agatha said, sitting back and folding her arms. "You wanted to warn me to steer clear of Wilkes and his 'attempted murder' case?"

"He knows we're friends," Bill said, laying his hands on the desk, "so he's being careful what he says around me, but I know from others that he's been making all sorts of threats about how he's going to throw the book at you if you step even slightly out of line on this one."

"He's a cretin," Agatha said with a sigh, "and he can't stop me from conducting an investigation, especially as the chamber of commerce is employing me to do so."

"Officially, I have to caution you against that, Agatha. Unofficially, I want to put the people who've been burgling the shops and who battered Aurelia Barclay behind bars. I can use any help you can give."

"Happy to oblige, but 'help' has to be a two-way street. I'll pass on anything that I think might be useful to you, but I want the same in return."

"Agreed—I'll do whatever I can on that front. Where have you got to so far?"

"Just scratching the surface. Sculley Security looks to be of interest, though."

"He installed the alarms on the burgled premises. He's been operating in the area for almost two years now. He's installed dozens of alarms, not just those that the burglars managed to get round."

"He must still be a suspect, though."

"Sure, but he has a pretty good alibi. He regularly travels down to London on business and he was away when every one of the burglaries happened. He has hotel receipts and we even have him on his London hotel's CCTV system."

"I'll be talking to him anyway," Agatha said. "I want to find out a bit more about him."

"Of course," Bill said, "but take it easy, Agatha. Don't go treading on Wilkes's toes, okay? Now, if you don't mind me asking, what's that little slip of paper with what looks like a poem written on it? You've looked at it at least a dozen times while we've been talking."

"Oh, it's just some nonsense that someone shoved through the letterbox. Some kind of prank, but it's irritating me. I hate the thought that someone is out there having a laugh at my expense."

She handed Bill the note and he read through it quickly, then looked across at Agatha with a sombre expression.

"Agatha, I think you need to take this seriously," he said, "and, as a police officer, I'm certainly taking it seriously."

"What are you talking about, Bill?"

"I've always been fascinated by little riddles like these, ever since I was a kid. I loved solving puzzles. An enquiring mind, you see? I guess it's what got me interested in becoming a police officer."

"So why are you so concerned about it?"

"Let's work it through together," Bill said, laying the paper on the table between them. "It's a letter puzzle. The title 'Your Final Case' sounds very Sherlock Holmesy but doesn't really mean much until you solve the rest of it.

"'Find me first in doors.' That's telling us to find the first letter of the solution in the word 'doors' and the first letter in 'doors' is, of course, 'D.'

"Then, 'See me weep for a second?' is asking us to look for the second letter, and the second letter in 'see,' 'me,' 'weep,' and 'second' is . . . ?"

"'E,'" Agatha answered.

"Exactly," Bill agreed. "Then we have 'I am in answer but not if you beckoned.' Well, there are four letters in 'answer' that aren't in 'if you beckoned.'"

"Umm . . . 'A,' 'S,' 'W,' and 'R.'"

"Spot on," Bill said. "So let's go with the first one, 'A.' Now we have 'The end of the cut is the fourth sign.'"

"'T' is the last letter in 'the cut,'" Agatha offered, warming to the theme.

"It is. So we're left with our last letter, which 'ends as your breath.'"

"'H'!" Agatha punched the air in triumph. "So that gives us D-E-A-T-H . . . death? My final case?"

Her face fell and Bill reached across the desk, laying his hand on hers.

"Agatha," he said gravely. "This is a death threat."

"Rubbish!" she said, snatching her hand away and banishing any such thoughts from her head. "This is someone's idea of a joke."

"I hope you're right," Bill said, "but there are plenty of people out there with good reason to bear a grudge against you. There are murderers locked up in prison because you tracked them down. I want you to take every precaution from now on. Don't go out anywhere on your own."

"That's just silly," she said, watching Bill photograph the note with his mobile phone. "I can't put my life on hold just because of a stupid note."

"I'm not asking you to do that," Bill said, tucking his phone back into his pocket. "You just need to be careful, okay? Promise me."

"All right!" Agatha threw her arms wide in exasperation. "I promise! I'll look twice before I cross the road and check under my bed every night for bogeymen!"

"Good," Bill said, rising to leave. "I'll make a few enquiries, but my guess is that this is probably just someone trying to scare you."

"Well, you know me better than that, Bill Wong," she replied, walking round the desk to hug him goodbye. "I don't scare that easily."

Agatha returned to her desk, made a few phone calls, then strode out into the main office.

"I've told Mr. Mason we'll take on the burglars," she

said. "Toni, you and I need to meet with him tomorrow to discuss our plan of action. Roy, we need to do likewise with Charles. Now . . . why are you all looking at me like that?"

The team were all staring silently at her, their expressions deadly serious.

"When Bill left he said we should keep our eyes open for any suspicious characters," Toni said.

"I told him we're usually the suspicious characters lurking around," Simon said, trying but failing to force a grin. "What's going on, boss?"

"Are you in some kind of trouble, Agatha?" Roy asked.

"Is it something to do with that note on your desk?" Patrick got straight to the point.

"Detectives," Agatha said, looking round the room and shaking her head. "You all think you're on to the case of the century, but I'm sorry to disappoint you— this is just a load of crap."

She explained about the note.

"A death threat?" Roy's right hand clutched at the neck of his pink paisley-pattern shirt.

"It's not the first time someone's threatened to kill me," Agatha said, waving aside their concern, "although usually they've got the balls to do it to my face. Don't lose any sleep over this. I certainly don't intend to."

The end of the working day rolled round and, one by one, the Raisin Investigations staff drifted off home until only Agatha and Roy were left in the office.

"Agatha," he called, strolling towards her room. "I

need to pop out to the shops to pick up a few things before we head back to your place. I'll only be about half an hour and I'll lock the street door. My car is parked close to yours, so wait here for me and we can walk round to the car park together."

"Roy," she said, stony-faced. "I'm a big girl. I can look after myself. Stop fussing."

"Very well," he said, turning on his heel. "I shall be back in half an hour in any case."

Agatha spent a few minutes sifting through tedious paperwork, paced three times round the office, then pulled on her coat, ready to leave. She would meet Roy downstairs. That would give her the chance to admire her clock in Mr. Tinkler's window. She wanted to photograph it and ping the picture to John, somewhere in the western Mediterranean. The dancing couple, after all, in her mind's eye, was them.

Approaching the shop front, however, she could see no sign of her clock. The velvet stand on which Mr. Tinkler had so carefully placed it was empty. There was a light on inside the shop and when she stepped towards the door, she could see it was standing slightly ajar.

"Mr. Tinkler!" she called, pushing the door fully open. "Mr. Tinkler, are you there?"

She moved hesitantly into the shop. Why had Mr. Tinkler left the door open? That was odd. He never did that, especially when it was so cold outside. Agatha had the uneasy feeling that something was wrong.

"Mr. Tinkler, I wanted to photograph the clock," she said loudly, making her way slowly forward past an ornate cast-iron umbrella stand loaded with a collection of silver-topped walking sticks. She pulled one of the sticks from the stand, felt its comforting heaviness and held it in front of her, like a club.

"Mr. Tinkler, are you . . . ?" She rounded the ornate screen to find the shopkeeper slumped in one of the leather armchairs, his face battered and bruised, trickles of blood at his nose and the corner of his mouth. "Mr. Tinkler!"

She dropped the stick and rushed forward, shouting in his face while gently feeling first at his neck and then his wrist, but there was no trace of a pulse.

Mr. Tinkler was dead.

Chapter Four

Agatha was sitting in the vacant armchair, staring at the shopkeeper's lifeless form, her phone in her hand, when a uniformed police officer, two paramedics and Roy Silver all arrived at once. The paramedics rushed over to the body and, on seeing Roy swoon, Agatha stood to let him have the seat. The police officer, a tall young man Agatha didn't recognise, stood beside her.

"You're Agatha Raisin, aren't you?" he asked.

"Yes, yes, that's me, Constable." Agatha was intently watching the paramedics, desperately hoping that they would be able to perform some kind of miracle that would open Mr. Tinkler's eyes and bring him back. It was not to be. They looked towards the police officer, sadly shaking their heads.

"Was it you who discovered the body, Mrs. Raisin?" asked the officer.

"Yes, it was," she said. "I just popped in to see him. We were at an auction with him this afternoon. We had tea sitting in those chairs . . ." Agatha could feel a tear welling in the corner of her eye but fought the urge to cry, her temper rising to force any feelings of grief or shock aside. "Who could have done this to him? Mr. Tinkler wouldn't harm a fly. He was a gentle soul. Who on earth would want to kill him?"

"That's what these gentlemen are here to find out, Mrs. Raisin," said the officer, looking towards the shop door where DCI Wilkes had appeared with Bill Wong in his wake. "If you would wait here, I'll let them know it was you who called it in."

The young policeman had a brief word with Wilkes before being sent outside to help a colleague stretching blue-and-white police tape across the front of the shop.

"Agatha Raisin," Wilkes said, striding towards her with a sneer on his face. "Here you are again, sticking your nose into police business and causing trouble."

"Have a heart, sir," said Bill. "Agatha knew Mr. Tinkler, after all."

"When I want your opinion, Sergeant," Wilkes said, giving Bill a dark look, but pointing at Agatha, "I'll ask *her* for it! She always seems to know more about police business than she should and I hear you two were having a cosy little chat earlier this afternoon. If I find out that you've been passing privileged information to this woman, Wong, I'll have you back in uniform on permanent nightshift before you can say 'blabbermouth'!"

"You're such a moron, Wilkes!" Agatha growled.

"Maybe you should be concentrating on this crime scene rather than all the petty crap that's rattling around inside your thick, empty skull!"

"I have years of experience in evaluating crime scenes, you stupid woman!" Wilkes spat. "I'm not an untrained blunderer like you! I can tell at a glance what's happened here. It's those damned shop burglars again. After the vicious assault on Audrey Bartlet—"

"I think you mean Aurelia Barclay, sir," Bill pointed out.

"Don't interrupt me, Sergeant! The burglars' behaviour has clearly escalated from straightforward theft to serious assault and now to murder. Mark my words, these are the exact same perpetrators."

"That's total bollocks!" Agatha cried, a flash of fury in her bear-like eyes. "If you assume this was done by the same people, you haven't a hope in hell of catching poor Mr. Tinkler's murderers!"

"I will conduct my investigations as I see fit!" roared Wilkes.

"And you'll get nowhere, as usual!" Agatha yelled back at him. "This is a completely different crime from the burglaries. The thieves who raided the shops were after small, easily portable, high-value items. They were in and out of premises before anyone knew they were there. Aurelia was hurt only because she was unfortunate enough to startle them and get in their way as they fled. What happened to Mr. Tinkler is nothing like that! Look at him! He's been beaten! And this shop is nothing like their usual targets. Mr. Tinkler didn't sell the sort of goods these burglars are after. The only thing that's missing here is . . . my clock . . ."

"*Your* clock?" Wilkes eyed her suspiciously. "*You* owned something that has been stolen from these premises this evening?"

"Well, I don't know for certain that it's been stolen," Agatha said, "but it's not where I expected it to be."

"Is that so?" Wilkes snorted. "This raises all sorts of questions about your involvement in events here, Mrs. Raisin. Take her down to the station, Wong. I'll deal with her when I'm finished here."

"Sir, you can't just—" Bill started to object, but Wilkes dismissed him with a wave of his hand.

"Just do as you're told, Sergeant," he said. "Mrs. Raisin will be voluntarily helping us with our investigation, and if she chooses not to, I can think of a number of very good reasons to take her into custody."

"Let's go, Bill," Agatha said, almost relieved to be able to escape from the despicable Wilkes. "I've been through this before. I'd rather just get it over with."

Roy insisted on going with Agatha and the three left the shop to the sound of Wilkes barking instructions at the recently arrived pathologist and the forensics team.

It was after ten at night by the time Agatha and Roy returned to her cottage in Lilac Lane. Having sat around at Mircester Police Station, answered countless questions put to her by Wilkes, then sat around some more, Agatha was tired and sorely irritated. Her front door opened as they walked up the path to reveal James

Lacey, her former husband—now her next-door neighbour and most trusted friend—standing inside.

"You must be exhausted after all that's happened,
my dear," he said, welcoming her inside and helping
her off with her coat. "Roy has been phoning regularly
to update me about everything. I didn't think you'd
want to come home to an empty house, so I let myself in
with the spare key. I can scarcely believe Wilkes put you
through all that, especially after the shock of finding Mr.
Tinkler."

"I can't get over the sight of him slumped in that
chair," Agatha said, reaching down to stroke her cats,
who were strutting around her ankles. "The poor man
never did anything to deserve that." She straightened
up, a look of solid determination on her face. "Whoever
killed him is going to regret it. I'll find them and they'll
get what's coming to them!"

"Let's not think too much about that tonight, Agatha,"
Roy said, resting a hand gently on her shoulder. "We can
talk to Bill in the morning. He'll make more sense of it
all than Wilkes ever will. Why that man had to badger
you with all those questions this evening is beyond me."

"I was the one who discovered the body," Agatha
said. "Wilkes couldn't ignore the fact that his enquiry
had to start with me, even though he hates me."

"He didn't have to do all that tonight, though," Roy
said. "He was just trying to lord it over you. He's pathetic. I was sitting in the reception area when he came
past, putting his coat on. He only stopped questioning
you because it was the end of his shift and he was off
home for his supper."

"Speaking of supper," James said, "I've already eaten, but I made a cottage pie for you both. I know it's a little late to eat but I thought you'd be starving by the time you got home."

"You're an angel," Agatha said, giving James a weary hug. "You too, Roy. Knowing that you were waiting to bring me home helped keep me going through all those pointless questions. Thank you both."

"The cottage pie smells delicious!" Roy said, rubbing his hands with glee and making for the kitchen with James. Picking up her mail from her little hall table, Agatha tried to push all thoughts of Mr. Tinkler out of her mind. She followed the two men, marvelling at the way they were getting along. James had never been comfortable around Roy when she had first introduced them. He had always found him too colourful, too flamboyant. As a former army officer, James had rigidly set ideas about how things should be done, how things should look and how people should behave. Roy didn't fit in with James's way of thinking.

Roy, of course, despite his irresistible charm and his undeniable ability to make friends wherever he went, had never much enjoyed James's company in the past, either. James had been too straightlaced for him, too much of a stickler for the rules and, in Roy's eyes, too plain boring. Roy might often appear to make friends, but sometimes his friendship went only skin deep. He chose very carefully those he treasured as real friends, and James had never been one of the chosen. Yet here they both were, chatting happily like old chums. How had that happened?

James had certainly changed since suffering from a brain tumour that had almost taken his life. He was a little more mellow these days, and the tensions that had caused such strife between him and Agatha when they were married had all but evaporated now they had agreed that they liked each other best as friends. Maybe Roy had cottoned on to that. He had, without doubt, become more tolerant of others and less sensitive over the years, but that hardly seemed enough to foster a friendship between these two. What, after all, did they have in common? Agatha smiled. *Me*, she thought to herself. *They're both here for* me, *both supporting* me! The sudden thought that both men cared about her gave her a warm glow inside and she hurried through to join them in the kitchen, where she opened a bottle of wine.

Agatha flicked through her mail while Roy poured each of them a glass of pinot noir. There were a couple of bills, the usual flyers and, to her horror, a square envelope with her name handwritten in the same neat capital letters as the one she had received at the office. Roy saw her staring at the envelope.

"It's another one, isn't it?" he said, trying not to sound alarmed.

"Another what?" asked James, his hands cocooned in oven gloves as he set the dish of cottage pie on the table.

"It's nothing," Agatha said, handing him the unopened envelope. "It's just someone messing around. Nothing to worry about."

James took the envelope and, with Agatha's approval, carefully slit it open with a kitchen knife. There was a single piece of paper inside, bearing a handwritten note just as before.

<u>WHO AM I?</u>

GIVEN TIME YOU'RE SURE TO MEET ME

YOU CANNOT HIDE OR CHEAT OR BEAT ME

YOU MUST FACE ME ALL THE SAME

AND AT THE END YOU'LL KNOW MY NAME

James read the rhyme aloud then frowned.

"You say you had another one of these?" he asked, and Agatha, who had already fished the first note out of her handbag in anticipation, handed it to him, explaining what Bill Wong had said.

"Well, I agree with Bill," James said, comparing the two slips of paper. "The first riddle is a death threat, but so is the second."

"It is?" Roy squeaked, holding a hand to his face.

"Just as 'death' was the answer to the first riddle, so it is with this one," James said. "The title, 'Who Am I?' can best be answered with 'Death' or 'The Grim Reaper,' call him what you will, once you've read through the riddle. The first line talks about being 'sure to meet me' and 'given time' . . . well, we all meet death eventually.

"The second line, obviously, says that we can't hide from death, cheat death or beat death. The third line says how we must all face death and the last line is saying that, ultimately, we all know death. Except, of course, this is addressed to you, Agatha. The writer is talking directly to you. Someone is threatening to kill you."

"Rubbish," Agatha said, serving Roy a large portion of cottage pie and helping herself to an even bigger one. "It's nonsense. Whoever sent those notes doesn't even know me."

"He knows where you work," Roy said, toying with his own food while watching Agatha devour a mouthful of hers. "Now, it seems, he knows where you live, too."

"Roy," Agatha said, swallowing hard. "It's very easy to find people in this country, providing that they're not actively trying to hide from you. I am among the easiest to find. I advertise my business—the place where I work—and there are any number of ways to find where I live, from looking me up in an online telephone directory to simply following me home."

"Agatha, I don't think you're taking this very seriously," James said. "He could be a real threat."

"You've both made the same mistake," Agatha pointed out, once she finished another taste of the cottage pie. "This is absolutely delicious, by the way, James. I would ask for your recipe, but you know I would only ruin it. For goodness' sake, eat up, Roy, before it goes cold."

"What mistake?" Roy asked, before finally trying the food, then nodding and, his mouth full, giving James a thumbs-up.

"You both said 'he,'" Agatha explained. "There's nothing in either of those notes that identifies the writer as a man."

"That may be true," James agreed, "but he . . . or whoever . . . could still be dangerous."

"I doubt it," Agatha said, enjoying a sip of wine. "Whoever's behind this is a complete amateur."

"What makes you say that?" Roy asked. "Why an amateur and how can you be sure that he . . . the riddler . . . doesn't know you?"

"The riddles are intended to frighten or intimidate me," Agatha said. "I'm not sure why the person who sent them wants to scare me, but if that person knew me, they'd know that I don't scare so easily. Why an amateur? Because both notes were hand delivered, and delivering a note here, to my house, means that whoever did so will have been caught by the security camera covering my front door. We can take a look at the footage to see who it is once we've finished eating. Really, James, the cottage pie is wonderful!" She spooned another large helping onto her plate.

Once they had finished eating, James cleared the table, Roy poured some more wine and Agatha brought her laptop into the kitchen.

"I can download the security camera recordings onto here," she said, tapping a few keys and scrolling through on-screen menus.

"I'm impressed," James said. "You've never been so comfortable with technology in the past."

Agatha shot him a resentful look.

"I have always been perfectly capable with computers and suchlike . . ." she began, but hesitated when Roy began to giggle.

"Only when punching the buttons harder and harder and swearing at the keyboard made it work." He chuckled.

"I am not beyond learning how to handle electronic gadgets," she said, pursing her lips. "Simon and Toni showed me how to do this. Young people take to this sort of thing like it's second nature to them, but old . . . I mean . . . more experienced people can get far more from it once they know the ropes.

"Now, I doubt even an amateur would risk being seen delivering a note like that in daytime, so we can start looking after dark. Now we just need to fast-forward and . . . look! That must be our suspect walking up the path!"

The image showed a figure in a dark anorak, with the hood up, clearly carrying the envelope in his hand.

"I'd say you two were right about it being a man," Agatha said. "You can tell by the way he moves. It doesn't look like a young man and . . . there!" She hit the keyboard to pause the footage when the man's face came into view. Just as she had predicted, the man was middle-aged. He was wearing black-framed glasses and was clean-shaven.

"Do you know him?" James asked.

"Never seen him before in my life," Agatha replied. "I can take this image and print it out at work. I'll let all the staff have a copy and tell them to keep their eyes peeled for this creep hanging around anywhere near the office."

"You should give a copy to Bill Wong, too," Roy suggested. "He might know who the riddler is."

"I suppose so," Agatha said reluctantly, "but I don't want anyone wasting time on this. I think the 'Who Am I?' note shows that this nutter wants to play games. It may be couched like a death threat, but he really wants me to try to find out who he is. He thinks he can outwit me, but I've no time for that sort of larking about."

"You're right," Roy agreed. "We've got a lot on our plates at the moment."

"Even more now," Agatha said. "We're going after whoever killed Mr. Tinkler. These were not the burglars who've been raiding other businesses, despite what Wilkes says."

"Why are you so sure?" James asked.

"Because Mr. Tinkler didn't sell the sort of things they've been stealing. He liked furniture and mirrors and cut crystal," Agatha said. "He didn't deal in jewellery or high-end watches or electronics."

"Maybe they were after cash," Roy said.

"Maybe," Agatha said, then shook her head. "I doubt if Mr. Tinkler would have had much cash on the premises. They wouldn't have targeted him for that. They'd have got more cash if they'd hit the sandwich shop round the corner."

"Do we know if anything was actually stolen?" James asked.

"I suppose we won't know that for sure until there's some kind of stock check," Agatha said. "The only thing we know for certain is missing, is my clock. Somehow, that clock holds the key. Find the clock, and we'll find the killers."

Early the following morning, Agatha put the final touches to her make-up and checked herself out in the full-length mirror in her bedroom. When she had woken that morning and flung open her curtains, she had been greeted with the sound of birdsong and a blue sky with only a few benign, high-flying fluffy clouds. Spring, it seemed, was finally starting to make its presence felt.

In tribute to the change in the weather, she had chosen a sky-blue suit with a knee-length sheath skirt and paired it with a pale-pink blouse. She had bought the suit some years before on a trip to Paris, shopping in her favourite Rue Saint-Honoré, allowing herself a strict budget, which she had, as always, blown completely in less than an hour. She hadn't worn this outfit in quite some time and had banished it to the back of a wardrobe when it had started to feel a little too tight. Had she not loved the cut and style of the jacket so much, it would have followed countless other outfits to a charity shop, but she was glad she hadn't disposed of it, especially as it now seemed to fit her better than ever.

Had she lost some weight? Of course she had! Even last night's cottage pie couldn't change that. She turned sideways, straightening her shoulders and sucking in her tummy. She'd been exercising every morning—well, almost every morning. The rolled exercise mat in the corner of the room caught her eye. She had to keep herself trim for her next rendezvous with John. She wanted to look her best in the summery dresses she had bought and to be fit for nights spent dancing and . . . her eyes wandered over to the bed . . . for all their other nocturnal activities. She sighed. The image of Mr. Tinkler slumped in the chair in his shop forced its way into her mind. Her reunion with John in Mallorca would have to be cancelled. Finding whoever had murdered Mr. Tinkler was now her top priority.

She stepped across to the bedroom door and opened it to be confronted by Roy, who had just opened the door to the spare bedroom opposite. He was wearing a sky-blue suit teamed with a pale-pink shirt. Even had they been trying, they couldn't have better matched their outfits.

"Agatha!" He beamed. "Good morning! I . . . oh . . ."

"No," she said, abruptly. "This won't do. We look like two flight attendants. We have people we need to see today and we can't meet anyone dressed like this."

"Ah . . ." Roy said, his smile fading slightly but quickly returning when he realised this gave him the chance to choose another outfit. "Not to worry! I have the perfect solution! Be with you in a moment."

Agatha doubted that. It never ceased to amaze her that, when sharing her home and her only bathroom with Roy, he consistently demonstrated that he took even longer to get himself ready than she did.

"I'll make some coffee," she said. "You make it snappy."

Roy took only slightly longer to change than Agatha had hoped, eventually appearing in the kitchen wearing a Prince of Wales checked suit. They drank their coffee, neither mentioning the events of the previous evening, then set off in Agatha's car for their first appointment of the day.

Talking through their plans for the Great Barfield Extravaganza en route to Barfield House helped Agatha to push the murder of Mr. Tinkler and the disappearance of her clock out of her thoughts. The urgency of the Barfield bash meant it was something they had to keep moving forward. She gripped the steering wheel tightly, using the imminent discussion with Charles as a useful distraction, vowing to focus a fresh, clear mind on avenging Mr. Tinkler once the extravaganza's wheels were in motion.

The morning sunshine had held, promising that an early Cotswold spring might indeed be on the way, and when Agatha parked her car where Barfield's long driveway opened up in front of the house, she spotted yellow and purple irises poking their heads through the grass at the edge of the lawn.

They walked up the flight of stairs leading to Barfield's giant front door and Roy knocked forcefully. He winced, blew on his hand and rubbed it vigorously, having made no noticeable sound rapping on the solid oak, iron-studded door that was several inches thick. Agatha gave him a look of mock sympathy and reached towards the bell-push in the doorframe. Before she could ring it, the door swung open and Gustav stood before them.

"Can I help you?" he asked, with a blank expression,

making the question sound neither like an offer of assistance nor any kind of welcome.

"Don't mess us about, Gustav," Agatha said, stepping forward. "I'm here to see Charles."

"I shall endeavour to ascertain whether Sir Charles is at home," Gustav offered, but Agatha already had one foot over the threshold and brushed past him.

"No need," she said. "I phoned earlier. We're expected."

"Yes, we're expected," Roy repeated, breezing past Gustav with an impish grin.

"Tolerated and endured are other words one might use," Gustav said through gritted teeth.

"Oooooh . . . miaowwww!" Roy said, turning to make a cat-claw gesture before following Agatha across the grand hall towards the library.

"Aggie, so good of you to come at a time like this," Charles said, rising from his desk to meet her at the door with a warm hug.

"What do you mean?" she asked, wriggling free and choosing to ignore the "Aggie."

"Well, you must be devasted by what happened to Mr. Tinkler," he said.

"How did you know about that already?" Agatha asked suspiciously.

"Front page of the *Mircester Telegraph*," Charles explained, retrieving the newspaper from his desk.

"Ah, yes, of course," Agatha said, scanning the story beneath the headline SAVAGE MIRCESTER MURDER. She hadn't taken the time to read the papers that morning and had scarcely listened to the radio. She folded the paper and handed it back to Charles, determined not to let the murder dominate her thoughts again.

"If you want to leave our discussions for another day . . ." Charles offered.

"No, we have time against us, after all," Agatha said briskly. "It's business as usual."

"Does 'business as usual' include finding Timothy Tinkler's murderer?" came the unmistakably reedy tone of Mrs. Tassy. She was standing in the library doorway, her own copy of the *Mircester Telegraph* tucked under her arm.

"It most certainly does," Agatha assured her, slightly taken aback by the use of the name "Timothy." She had never known Mr. Tinkler's first name. She abandoned any effort at suppressing thoughts of the murder. It was too big a thing to keep shutting it out. "You sound like you knew him."

"I met him when he was just a young chap," Mrs. Tassy said, gliding towards her usual armchair by the window. "I attended an antiques fair in St. Jude's church hall in Carsely. He cautioned me against buying a rather attractive silver dish, which he advised me was silver plate, although it claimed to be solid silver."

"Just as well," Gustav said, appearing with a tray of coffee cups. "Sir Charles would probably have flogged it during the hard times along with the rest of the family silver."

"After that," said the old lady, "he visited the house on a number of occasions to help in valuing various items, mainly furniture, for insurance purposes. He was a shy little man but quite charming in his own way. Related to the Telford Tinklers, as I understand it."

"I wish I'd taken the time to get to know him better," Agatha said. "We'd really only started to become friends."

"Speaking of friends," Charles said breezily, determined to change the subject, "bring another cup, would you, Gustav? Claudette will be joining us shortly."

Right on cue, Claudette Duvivier dashed into the room, throwing her arms around Agatha and kissing her once on each cheek.

"Agatha, you must tell me how are you?" she demanded breathlessly, her melodic French accent desperate with concern. "This has been such an awful thing to have happen."

"It's good to see you, Claudette." Agatha took a step back and looked the young Frenchwoman up and down. She was wearing a simple white polo shirt with the logo of the vineyard she owned in France embroidered neatly on the breast. Her long dark hair hung straight and glossy to her shoulders and her olive skin against the polo shirt gave her the healthy, fresh look of someone who enjoyed being outdoors. "You look fantastic, as always."

"And you also," Claudette said, running her fingers down the lapel of Agatha's jacket. "This is *très chic*. It is French, *non*?"

"You two really should join each other's fan clubs," Charles said, smiling. "Let's take a seat and have some coffee. I'd like Claudette to sit in on our discussion, Agatha. She's been advising on our Château Barfield and fitting in some show-jumping matches at the same time."

"Events, Charles, not 'matches,'" Agatha corrected him.

"Yes, yes, of course," Charles said, waving for Gustav to pour the coffee. "In any case, we have our very own event to talk about."

Agatha and Roy ran through their thoughts on how the launch for Château Barfield should work, describing the whole extravaganza in detail and passing Charles a schedule for the day.

"This all looks great," he said, with a slight hesitation. "But food stalls outdoors as well as catering indoors? Steam traction engine rides? Hot-air balloon rides? Would we expect people to pay for these things?"

"We can't charge for the tethered-balloon experience," Roy explained, "because special passenger licences would be needed, but we aim to have sponsors covering most of those sorts of costs."

"People will also be able to make a donation to charity instead of paying for things like that," Agatha said. "I also want to stage a charity auction later in the day, so we'll want all of your posh chums with those big country houses to donate items for the auction. All they need do is to have a rummage in the attic, or get their butlers to do it for them."

Gustav glowered at her through narrowed eyes.

"I'm sure we can persuade people to dust off a few less-loved family heirlooms and whatnot," Charles said, scanning the schedule. "We've got a lot of ideas here. Can you pull it all together in time?"

"We can make it work," Agatha said, with solid confidence.

"I mean, even with this dreadful Tinkler business?" Charles said.

"We'll make it happen," Agatha assured him.

"Then let's go for it," Charles said, and they spent the next half an hour talking through the details. Charles's aunt said nothing at all during the discussion, although Agatha was aware that the old lady was watching her closely. It wasn't until the conversation drew to a close that she spoke up.

"According to the newspaper, Mrs. Raisin," she said, "you were the one who found Timothy's body."

"I was," Agatha confirmed, "and I intend to be the one to find his killer."

"That's very reassuring," said Mrs. Tassy. "You're really rather good at that sort of thing, aren't you? It's always heartening to have good people dealing with important matters."

"That must have been how Lady Juliana felt about William Harrison," Agatha said, turning to Charles. "She had a good, reliable person there to deal with important matters."

"Still pondering over that old mystery?" Charles asked.

"You know me, Charles," Agatha said. "I like to get to the bottom of things."

"Well, I should imagine Lady Juliana felt hugely relieved to have Harrison working for her," Charles said. "She needed someone running the estate she could trust implicitly."

"Did anyone ever check out his story about being abducted and making his way back to England?"

"That would have been very difficult to do," Charles said. "Clearly whoever kidnapped him and sold him into slavery wouldn't want to stand up in front of a magistrate and admit to what they'd done. Neither was there any record of him taking passage aboard a ship when he made his way back to England. When his master died, Harrison said he tried to persuade several sea captains to take him, but they all refused. Eventually, he used a golden bowl given to him by his old master to bribe a crewman to help him stow away. The sailor hid him aboard ship and brought him food during the voyage. Once he was in London, of course, he was able to contact people he knew."

"I see . . ." Agatha said, frowning. "So the only corroboration of his story starts in London."

"As far as I know," said Charles.

They said their goodbyes, Claudette insisting on meeting Agatha for lunch at some point before she had to return to her estate in the Gironde.

Mrs. Tassy stood beside her nephew, watching Agatha's car disappear down the avenue of rhododendrons leading to the main gate.

"Well, Charles, you must be feeling very pleased with yourself," she said quietly.

"What do you mean?" he asked.

"Mrs. Raisin has taken your bait. She is now busier than ever with a real murder to solve on top of that old Campden Wonder mystery."

"Yes, she made a point of asking about that, didn't she?" Charles smiled and stuck his hands in his trouser pockets. "She's like a dog with a bone. Several bones, it now appears, and she won't leave any of them alone. We're going to be seeing a lot more of her here over the next few weeks—and *here* is just where I want her."

"You should be careful of your fingers," Gustav said gravely, while gathering the coffee cups onto a tray. "I believe that's the customary advice to offer little boys who play with fire."

Claudette, standing unnoticed in the doorway after waving Agatha off, turned without saying a word and made her way upstairs to her room.

Agatha bustled into the office, accepting the usual armful of paperwork from Helen and asking her to book a meeting with Martin Randall at his auction house. Roy reminded her that they were going out to meet two potential sponsors and the president of the local vintage-vehicle society that afternoon, and Toni followed her to her room.

"Bill Wong will be round to see you shortly," she said, "and I've arranged for us to see Stuart Sculley from the security company tomorrow morning. Patrick is on the first night patrol this evening with one of his old police pals, Simon is keeping an eye on Mrs. Parker and I've almost finished those background checks."

"Excellent," Agatha said. "I'm sending you an image of a man who stuck another one of those ridiculous riddle notes through my door."

"You've had another one?" Toni looked alarmed.

"Don't worry, Toni, it's all a load of nonsense," Agatha said, "but if you can print out his picture, everyone can keep their eyes peeled for the little toad. Maybe you can

show it to people in the pub across the lane, too. Somebody might recognise him."

"Okay," Toni said. "I was going to ask to take a look at
their security-camera footage as well. They might have
images of whoever went into Mr. Tinkler's shop . . ."

"Good idea," Agatha agreed. "Bill will already have
asked them for it, but they're bound to have a copy we
can take a look at."

Agatha busied herself with paperwork and phone
calls for the next hour or so until Bill Wong knocked
lightly on her door. She welcomed him in and they sat
down to talk.

"Does Wilkes know you're here?" Agatha asked. "He
really doesn't want us speaking to each other."

"I know, but you're an important witness and you had
something stolen from the shop. Do you have a photograph of the clock?"

"I wish I did. It was gone when I went down to the
shop yesterday evening and . . ." She paused, the image
of Mr. Tinkler in the armchair flashing back into her
mind.

"Okay, we'll go with the description that you gave to
Wilkes for now," Bill said quickly, "and maybe the auction
house will have a photo if they put it in a catalogue. Now,
Toni told me when I arrived that you've had another note."

"Yes," Agatha said with a sigh, hauling her handbag
out of her desk drawer and finding the "Who Am I?"
riddle for Bill.

"Have you any idea at all who might be writing
these?"

"No, but I've got a picture of him," Agatha said,

waving Toni into the room, who delivered a couple of prints of the security-camera image before leaving again.

"Can't say I recognise him," Bill said, "but I'll ask Toni to send me the image and I can spread it around to see if anyone knows him."

"You shouldn't waste time on this moron, Bill. We need to concentrate on Mr. Tinkler's murder."

"No, 'we' do not," Bill said. "You are much too close to this, Agatha. Officially I have to warn you to leave the murder investigation to the police."

"And unofficially?"

"Unofficially . . ." Bill spread his arms in exasperation, then shook his head, smiling in resignation. "Unofficially, I know you'll do exactly as you want. Just keep me informed and stay out of Wilkes's way."

Having spent the afternoon in Barfield meetings with Roy, Agatha returned to the office alone, Roy taking off to visit his friend Tamara, who ran riding stables near Blockley. Working late, Agatha eventually walked out into the main office to find Toni the only one still there. They decided to pop into the King Charles for a drink before going home, chatting as they walked down the stairs to the gloom of the old lane, where the woefully inadequate streetlights cast ripples of shadow across the cobbles.

Agatha was surprised to see that the police tape had gone from around the antiques shop, which stood in darkness. Turning to Toni to mention the missing tape, she saw a grey van roaring up the deserted lane, screeching to a halt beside them. A side door slid open and a masked man dressed entirely in black leaped out, grabbing hold of Toni from behind. Agatha lunged forward to help Toni fight him off but the driver of the van was suddenly there, wrapping one arm round her waist and clamping his gloved hand over her mouth.

Toni screamed, dropped her handbag then flung back her head, making solid contact with her attacker's nose.

Agatha struggled against her own opponent, wrenched her head to one side, felt a finger across her mouth and bit it as hard as she could while stamping down with her leg, driving the high heel of her shoe like a spike into the bridge of her assailant's foot. He roared in pain and Agatha pushed herself away from him.

Toni wriggled free from her dazed attacker, turning and swinging her leg in one swift movement, kicking him hard in the groin. He doubled over with a wheezing whimper, falling back into the van. The antiques shop's lights came on and the van driver immediately hopped back behind the wheel, gunning the engine, the van then careering off down the lane.

"Snakes and bastards!" Agatha gasped, breathing hard, her hands on her knees. "Toni . . . you okay?"

"I think so," Toni replied, out of breath and crouching to pick up her handbag.

"Mrs. Raisin," came a man's voice. "Please do come inside."

A sudden chill seeped down Agatha's spine, leaving her frozen with horror. Standing on the pavement in the yellow light of the shop window was Mr. Tinkler!

Chapter Five

Agatha backed away from the apparition, feeling Toni at her shoulder. She pointed, staring at the face, and the familiar, misty green eyes looked back at her over half-moon glasses.

"But . . . but you're dead!" was all she could say.

"Clearly not," said Mr. Tinkler, holding out a hand towards her and gesturing towards the shop door with the other. "I assure you I am very much alive. Please do come inside. You both look like you've had a nasty shock."

"Don't do it!" Toni whispered, then repeated, "Don't do it! Don't . . ."

"Oh, be quiet, Toni!" Agatha hissed, studying Mr. Tinkler's face. The fact that he was there at all was very wrong but, concentrating on his appearance, there were other nagging details that didn't make sense. His hairline was ever so slightly different. His features looked a little less chubby. There were small, erroneous wrinkles at the corners of his eyes and faint lines each side of his mouth. She relaxed and took a step towards him.

"Thank you, Mr. Tinkler," she said, calmly. "That would be very kind."

"Agatha, no!" Toni whispered, appalled. "You can't . . ."

Agatha reached behind her, grabbed Toni's wrist and dragged her into the shop, following Mr. Tinkler. He closed the door, locked it securely, then led them to the back section behind the decorative screen. The leather chairs were nowhere to be seen, having been replaced by solid, wooden dining chairs. Mr. Tinkler invited them to sit, explaining that he couldn't stand the sight of the leather chair his brother had died in, so he had moved both of them to the store in the back yard.

"So what should we call you?" Agatha asked. "Mr. Tinkler, after all, is the name I associate with your brother."

"Brother . . . ?" Toni frowned at Agatha.

"Mr. Tinkler mentioned he had a brother," Agatha said, "but he didn't tell me you were twins."

"Twins . . ." Toni's shoulders dropped and she sighed with relief.

"The resemblance is really quite remarkable," Agatha said. "I'm so sorry about your brother. We all are. He was a lovely man."

"Ah, yes, thank you," Mr. Tinkler said, then apologised. "I'm Tristan. I'm sorry if I startled you, but when I heard the commotion outside, I thought I should investigate. What exactly happened to you both?"

"Two men tried to abduct us," Agatha said bluntly.

"Good heavens!" Tristan was horrified. "We must call the police!"

Agatha looked towards Toni and, without saying a word, each gave a slight shake of her head.

"We don't need to call the police," Agatha said. "We'll catch up with those two eventually, no doubt."

"Why on earth would they want to kidnap you?"

"Right now, I've really no idea," Agatha replied, rubbing her hand across her forehead as if trying to straighten her thoughts. "I'd say they bit off more than they could chew, but things might have turned out differently if you hadn't switched on the shop lights, Tristan. That frightened them off. Beyond that, I'm struggling to think straight."

She looked up, caught sight of herself in an elaborate, gold-framed wall mirror and was devastated to see that the hand the van driver had slapped over her mouth had smeared her lipstick right across her cheek, creating a bizarre, oversized, lopsided grin.

"I'm sorry," she said, shooting to her feet and gripping her handbag, "but may I use your bathroom?"

"Yes, of course," Tristan said, standing as Agatha rushed past him to the door at the rear of the shop. "You must both be feeling awful. Let me find something to calm our nerves."

By the time Agatha had repaired her make-up, she returned to find Tristan and Toni sitting cradling crystal brandy balloons boasting a generous measure of amber liquid. Tristan stood, handed her a glass and raised his in a toast.

"To my brother, Timothy Tinkler . . ." he said, the two

women repeating the name, ". . . and to finding the bastards who murdered him!"

They drank through a short silence. Agatha watched Toni. She had calmed down, but seemed taken aback by Tristan's sudden vehemence, given how gently he had spoken up to that point. Agatha was less surprised at Tristan. He had, after all, just lost a brother—more than that, his twin. She then felt slightly guilty. The brandy was delicious and she silently scolded herself for feeling so pleased that it had banished the taste of the van driver's filthy glove from her mouth in the way that repeated sluicing with water in the bathroom had failed to do. Why did trivial thoughts like that elbow their way to the front of your mind when there were far more grave matters to consider?

"Couldn't agree more, Tristan," Agatha said. "In fact, Toni and I are already working on finding the killers."

"Ah, Toni . . ." said Tristan, as though he had just realised who the young woman with the blonde hair was. "Tim talked so much about you, Agatha, but he also mentioned you, Toni. 'The young apprentice is almost as formidable as her boss,' is how he put it."

"I didn't realise he was such a fan," Agatha said.

"He was a huge admirer of you, Agatha," Tristan said. "He talked about you a great deal. He was proud to have this shop immediately below the offices of Raisin Investigations."

"It's always been clear how proud he was of the shop," Agatha commented. "Antiques shops sometimes look like they're just stacked with junk, but he kept this place neat and orderly."

"Yes, that's why I ripped down all of that hideous police tape. Tristan would have hated having that blighting his shop."

"I wondered where that had gone," Toni said. "DCI Wilkes won't like you having meddled with his crime scene."

"They've been in here and done all their messing about," Tristan said. "Somehow I doubt they'll glean any advantage from it. If Wilkes wants his silly tape reinstated, he'll find it in my bin!"

He gave a slight cough, covering his mouth with one hand and rubbing a tear from his eye with the other.

"I still can't believe he's gone," he said quietly. "I feel like he's still here, still part of me, still with me, just like he has been since the day we were born."

"Did the police call to tell you what had happened?" Agatha asked.

"They did, but they didn't need to," Tristan replied. "I already knew. I knew something was wrong. It's a feeling we always had. I always knew when Tim was in trouble and he got that same feeling about me. It was a kind of anxious, unsettled notion that something was up. When that suddenly stopped and there was a terrible, black emptiness, I knew . . . I'd never felt that before . . . I knew he was dead. I was on my way back here when the police called, but they didn't need to tell me a thing. I told them the exact second that Tim died. He had a heart attack, you know. His poor old heart gave out when they started roughing him up."

"I'm so sorry for you," Toni said, tears rolling down her cheeks.

"You said you were on your way back here," Agatha noted. "Had you been here earlier?"

"Yes, I'd dropped by to see Tim earlier that afternoon, as I did from time to time."

"You visited regularly?" Agatha asked. "I'm surprised we haven't met before."

"Ah, but we have, Agatha." Tristan smiled. "I used to look after the shop when Tim was off on one of his buying trips, or on one of the foreign tours he liked to take. He loved Venice and Rome . . . When he was away, you and I often nodded a 'good morning' through the shop window as you passed by."

"Really? I would never have realised."

"People didn't. We've always looked so alike. When we were at school, the teachers couldn't tell us apart, so they split us up, putting us in different classes. That didn't do them any good at all. We used to go to each other's classes just for a laugh. No one ever knew. We even took each other's exams when we thought it would get us better grades!" He laughed, then wrung his hands. "We'll get them, won't we? Promise me we'll get the people who did this."

"We will, Tristan," Agatha said, her jaw set firm.

"Yes, we will," Toni said, screwing up a tissue she'd been using to dab her eyes. She shoved it into her coat pocket. "I've had a look at the security cameras at the King Charles. It shows two men dressed in black entering and leaving the shop."

"The same men who just attacked you two?" asked Tristan.

"Hard to tell," Toni said, producing her phone. "I've got the clip here on my phone."

Toni showed the grainy black-and-white video of two men dressed in black hoodies entering the shop, then fast-forwarded to the time when they could be seen running out the front door and off down the lane.

"I must have missed them by minutes," Agatha said.

"Are they the men from the van?" Tristan asked.

"Impossible to tell," Agatha said. "Scumbags dressed all in black seem to have been popping up all over the place recently burgling shops, then two guys in black tried to snatch us and those two on Toni's phone are our prime suspects for your brother's murder. I very much doubt if they're all the same people. Wait a minute . . . show us them leaving the shop again, Toni."

Toni rewound the video and Agatha squinted at it.

"Look at the way they're running when they come out," she said. "Neither of them is carrying anything. They don't have my clock."

"Oh, they didn't take your clock, Agatha," Tristan said. "I can assure you they don't have it."

"So who does have it?" Agatha asked.

"I do. That's why I visited earlier. Tim asked me to repair it. I took it home."

"You took the clock?" Agatha frowned. "It wasn't even in the shop—so what were these two after?"

"I've had a good look round," Tristan said. "Tim usually had some cash in a drawer in his table and the drawer is empty, so we can assume they took the money.

There wouldn't have been more than a few pounds, though. He'd have let them have that rather than . . ."

"Do you know if anything else is missing?" Toni asked.

"I don't think anything else was taken. Tim didn't really deal in items small enough to slip into a pocket—nothing of value that those two could run off with like that. So why did they do that to him?"

"We'll find that out when we get our hands on them," Agatha said. "I take it you've spoken to the police?"

"Only by telephone," Tristan replied. "Detective Sergeant Wong wants me to go in to see him tomorrow."

Agatha looked at him intently. The resemblance to his brother was quite incredible.

"You don't live anywhere near here, do you?" she asked.

"No, my place is just outside King's Lynn in Norfolk."

"That's about three hours by car," Agatha said, making a quick mental estimate. "Does anyone in Mircester know you? I mean, is there anyone in this area who knows about you and your brother being identical twins?"

"I doubt it," said Tristan with a shrug. "It isn't something that we tended to talk about with others. People ask too many silly questions."

"Do you have any friends around here?" Agatha asked.

"Not really. Tim had a few chums, mainly in the antiques business, but my friends are all in Norfolk."

"Then I need you to go home, Tristan. I'll square things with Bill Wong. If he needs to meet you, he'll take a trip to King's Lynn."

"Well, I'm happy to shut up the shop and go home," Tristan said. "Apart from anything else, I'd like to spend more time on your clock. I'm sure I can get it working again but the mechanism is quite peculiar. Working on it will certainly help to take my mind off things here, but why did you say you 'need' me to go?"

"Because of the way Toni and I reacted when we saw you," Agatha said. "We were terrified. I want to keep you a secret. I don't know how yet, but the best weapon in our armoury when it comes to catching your brother's killers may yet turn out to be the ghost of Timothy Tinkler!"

With Roy out to dinner, Agatha drove home to Carsely alone. On a summer day, the road that made its way down from the A44 into the village was like a long, joyous welcome arch, the branches of the trees on either side forming a tunnel with their foliage. The dappled shade, especially when the weather was warm, was a delight. At this time of year and this time of day, with the spring buds on the oak and beech trees still in their infancy and darkness blanketing the countryside, the welcome was gloomy rather than joyous.

Turning into Lilac Lane, she heard and felt a loud rumbling. Was there something wrong with the car? The noise came again and she realised it had nothing to do with her car—it was her stomach. She tutted. She knew she had food for the cats but was pretty sure she had nothing in the cupboard or the fridge to feed herself. James might be home, but she didn't want to bother him.

She needed a nice, quiet evening alone with the cats to think through everything that was going on. A visit to Harvey's, the village post-office-cum-general-store, was called for. They generally had a reasonable selection of frozen meals-for-one that could be nuked in the microwave and ready to eat in less than four minutes.

Leaving her car in its usual space outside her cottage, she walked back along Lilac Lane, passing the numerous lilac bushes that gave the street its name. Their branches spread out in the streetlight, displaying a profusion of buds and new shoots but, as yet, none of the spectacular flower spikes that would fill the air with scent in just a couple of months' time. That was something to look forward to and, in a different way, prompted by another burble from her stomach, so was her evening meal. She loved to eat well when good, wholesome food was cooked for her in a restaurant or at least by someone, such as James, who knew what they were doing. She had neither the patience to cook for herself nor even the inclination to learn how, but justified her frequent raids on Harvey's freezer section by assuring herself that frozen meals were made for busy people like her who had no time to spare for pottering in the kitchen. It never occurred to her that the manager of Harvey's kept the freezer stocked almost entirely for her benefit. The staff there knew her favourites almost as well as she did. Should she have the lasagne, the chicken curry, or maybe the fish pie? The answer became obvious when she turned into the high street. She'd have none of them. Harvey's was closed.

"Bugger . . ." Agatha muttered to herself. She hadn't

realised quite how late it was. Then she spotted a familiar figure striding along the pavement towards her.

"Good evening, Mrs. Raisin!" Margaret Bloxby, wife of Alf, the local vicar, gave Agatha a cheery wave.

"Good evening, Mrs. Bloxby," Agatha said, smiling. The two women were close friends, but it amused them in public to use the formal salutation that was preferred by the Carsely Ladies Society. Only in private, over a glass of wine or a schooner of sherry at the vicarage, were they Margaret and Agatha.

"I called at your place earlier," Margaret said, "but you were out."

"And I'm still out," Agatha said with a rueful smile. "Out of supplies more than anything. I lost track of the time and forgot that Harvey's would be closed."

"Well, you're in luck!" Margaret said, linking her arm into Agatha's. "I have a casserole in the oven that should be ready in about half an hour, and Alf is out to dinner with the bishop, so he won't be back until late. Come along. We've time for a glass of sherry before we eat."

"Actually, I . . ." For a moment, Agatha tried to pull away, but a look of good-natured reproach from Margaret forced her into submission. The vicarage was at the far end of the high street and within a few minutes she was sitting opposite Margaret by a gentle log fire, relaxing with a sherry.

"Sorry if I seemed a bit standoffish back there," Agatha said. "I thought I wanted an evening alone— you know, time to myself—but this is far better. This is heavenly."

"It's a vicarage," Margaret said, laughing, "so we're

still a couple of steps short of heaven, but I know what you mean. I love it here."

This was the room where they always sat to chat—Margaret's living room. The vicarage was an old building, not as old as the fourteenth-century church it stood next to, but old enough to have matured and evolved the kind of comforting character that made it such a sanctuary. The floorboards were uneven, occasionally sloping slightly, making you feel like you were walking along the moving deck of a ship. The armchairs they had sunk into had soft feather cushions that hugged you like old friends, and the faint scent of lavender furniture polish filtered through the comforting smell of the fire, creating a welcoming air of calming goodness. Not heaven, perhaps, Agatha thought, but certainly a haven from all the stresses and strains of the world outside.

"I called round earlier to see if you were all right," Margaret said. "That was a terrible business with the poor antiques man."

"It was," Agatha agreed. "In fact, that shop has been full of surprises these past two evenings."

She went on to describe how she and Toni had fought off their attackers but stopped short of telling Margaret about the Tinkler twins. That was something about which she had sworn Toni and Tristan to secrecy, and a secret shared, even with a good friend like Margaret, was a secret no longer.

"These men tried to kidnap you?" Margaret was becoming angry on Agatha's behalf. "That's outrageous! What did the police have to say?"

"Nothing so far," Agatha said. "We haven't told them.

We have too much going on right now to have the police trampling all over Raisin Investigations."

"What do you mean?"

"I've received two silly little riddles," Agatha said, pulling the notes from her handbag and handing them to her friend. "They appear to be death threats and they could be linked to what happened this evening. When those two goons tried to grab us, I think they were probably after me. Poor Toni just happened to be in the wrong place at the wrong time."

"In the right place at the right time, I would say. You wouldn't have been able to fight off two of them."

"You're right . . . I know. I feel guilty about it, too. Being with me put Toni in real danger."

"And not for the first time, Agatha, but don't fret too much about Toni. That young lady is a tough cookie. She works with you because she loves it. She loves the excitement and the thrill of it all. That's not something she had when you first met her. She was stacking shelves in a Mircester supermarket and trying to dodge her sleazy boss's roving hands."

"It's a good job I got her out of there," Agatha said with a soft laugh, "otherwise she'd eventually have battered him to bits with a frozen baguette."

"Who do you imagine might be behind these threats?"

"It could be any one of a number of lowlifes," Agatha said, taking a sip of her sherry. "Over the years, my investigations have meant a lot of marriages have ended in divorce, a lot of people have lost ill-gotten gains and a lot of people have ended up in jail."

"I can imagine there's a long list of suspects in your

case files. That's why you said the police would go 'trampling all over' your business."

"I want to avoid that at all costs. Some of our work is very sensitive—highly confidential. Having the police prying into it all would mean potential clients might give us a wide berth. That would be very bad for business."

"But these notes are so sinister . . . and a kidnap attempt . . ."

"You know, I'm not convinced they're definitely linked. The notes are meant to intimidate me. Whoever wrote them wants to play games. They want to tempt me into tracking them down and play me for a fool. That's something they'd want to string out for their own amusement. Abducting me puts an end to the game. It doesn't feel like the same person is behind the notes and the attack this evening."

"But that's worse, isn't it? That means there are two separate unknowns targeting you!"

"It seems that way. Still, those two goons made a real hash of things earlier. They'll make other mistakes, and every slip they make will bring us one step closer to them. We know they used a grey van, for example, although with its lights off we didn't get the registration. It could be on the King Charles's security camera. Toni will check that out tomorrow. As for the riddler, he or she will get cocky in the end and give the game away. I won't let any of them get the better of me."

"That's certainly not in doubt," Margaret said, heaving herself out of the soft chair. "The food will be ready. We can eat in the kitchen."

Over a dinner of chicken casserole, boiled potatoes and

broccoli, the two women chatted amiably about nothing in particular, avoiding what the TV and radio news were now calling the "Antiques Shop Murder" and any talk of death threats while enjoying a glass of crisp Chablis.

"Now, I know you're not one for gossip . . ." Margaret said, finishing a mouthful of casserole.

"Oh, be serious!" Agatha laughed. "My entire business revolves around gossip and who said what to so-and-so!"

"Well, of course," Margaret agreed, "but you need evidence to back up any claims that come from gossip. Not so the Carsely Ladies Bridge Club . . ."

She went on to tell how a scandal had erupted within the bridge club elite with Mrs. Frobisher and her bridge partner, Mrs. Nightingale, accusing Mrs. Nettles and Mrs. Alcock of falsifying their scores over the course of the winter tournament. As honorary president of the Ladies Society, Margaret explained how she had been dragged into the debate.

"I couldn't believe it at first," she said, "but they were all taking it terribly seriously. Mrs. Nightingale even demanded that we bring you in to investigate!"

"How did you resolve it?" Agatha asked, knowing how, with pride and reputation on the line, the dispute could easily have led to village feuds fuelled by ever more fruity gossip that would drag on for years, possibly generations. If she knew anything about the Carsely Ladies, it was that they had long memories.

"I didn't," Margaret said, laughing. "I told them to leave it with me and that, like Solomon, I would come to a decision in due course."

"Tell them to use their common sense and agree on the scores," Agatha advised, "otherwise you will declare all their matches void and they'll have to play them again. That way, the best players will come out on top, as they should. This really is delicious," she added, polishing off her casserole. "I wish I was a better cook. James made a fabulous cottage pie for Roy and me last night, but nothing I attempt ever works out the way it's meant to."

"Well, we all have different talents," Margaret said. "In just a few moments you've solved a problem I've been struggling with for days, so that sort of thing is definitely your bag more than cooking. How is James, by the way?"

"He seems fine. I'm glad that we're friends. It's better that way."

"I remember when he first came to Carsely. Now that really started the gossip mill grinding. The word around the village was that you would stop at nothing until you had the handsome Mr. Lacey's ring on your finger."

"Much as I hate to think I was the subject of so much tittle-tattle," Agatha said, shifting uncomfortably, "they were right. I was besotted with him, but now that we're no longer married, things are far less . . . volatile."

"Sir Charles must be pleased about that."

"What makes you say that?"

"Because it means he has one less rival to contend with."

"Oh, I don't think he's concerning himself about that anymore, Margaret. I've made it pretty clear that the days when he and I were together are long gone. We're now working closely, though, preparing for the launch of his wine business."

Agatha went on to describe how she and Roy were coordinating the Great Barfield Extravaganza and how she'd far rather be concentrating on that than any silly death threats.

"I want to make the Barfield event a huge success," she said. "Charles is determined that we should have fun doing it, too."

"Tread carefully with that one, Agatha. He's slowly drawing you back into his sphere of influence."

"I don't think I need worry about Charles in that way. He's not like he used to be. He's changed."

"Men like Sir Charles Fraith never really change. He regards women as the kind of trophies he and his top-drawer cronies acquire when they go hunting and shooting. He knows how easy it is to come by some conquests. I'm sure that pretty young things are dazzled by the wealth, the stately home and what they see as a glamorous lifestyle—caught like rabbits in his headlights. You, on the other hand, are the real challenge—the one he keeps losing, the greatest trophy of them all."

"You flatter me," Agatha said, beginning to feel more than a little perturbed by the way her friend was talking about Charles, "but I can handle him."

"Yes, I'm sure you can," Margaret said slowly. At heart she was a gentle, good person who would never wish anyone ill and she looked suddenly tired, as though the effort of decrying Charles's character had exhausted her. She reached for the wine bottle and smiled. "One for the road?"

"Why not?" Agatha held out her glass.

"Agatha! Agatha, wake up!" came the hushed voice.

She groaned, rolled over and felt the cats leap from the bottom of the bed. She knew it was Roy. It was, without doubt, his voice, but he sounded like he was in a desperate flap. She reached for the light on her bedside table.

"No—don't switch the light on! They'll see us!"

"What? What the hell are you talking about, Roy?" She moaned, yawning and shaking her head to clear the fuzziness of that final glass of Margaret's Chablis. She opened her eyes slightly to see Roy standing by her bed, wearing purple silk pyjamas and using a cupped hand to shield the light from the torch on his phone.

"I think there's someone sneaking around outside," Roy whispered. "I got up to use the bathroom and I swear I saw someone in the back garden."

Agatha was now wide awake.

"Pass me my dressing gown," she said, pointing to where it was draped over the chair by her dressing table, "and show me where you saw them."

They crept across the corridor into the spare room, where Roy extinguished his torch. "We can see outside better if there's no light in here," he said quietly.

"And they can't see in so well," Agatha agreed, peering out of the window down into the garden below. The moonlight had reduced the abundant shades of green in her small lawn and the surrounding shrubs to a flat palette of grey variations. Then she saw a shadow move in the shrubbery at the very back of the garden, and two black-clad figures eased their way through the bushes onto the grass. They were crouched low and, Agatha reasoned, could not be seen either from the windows of James's cottage or, because of her garden's layout, from any of her windows bar the one from which she was watching. She shrank back into the shadows a little when she saw one of them look up in her direction.

"They've come across the fields behind the house," Agatha whispered to Roy.

"I'll call the police," said Roy.

"Not yet!" Agatha insisted. "I want to get a better look at them. All they have to do is creep towards us a little further . . ."

The two figures obliged by making their way towards the house, hugging the shadows of the shrubs at the side of the lawn. Agatha could see that one of them was carrying a rucksack. Then, when they came within range of a discreetly placed sensor below the gutter above the kitchen window, in a flash the garden was returned to green, flooded with light from high-powered security lamps.

Agatha squinted at the two men in black. From the way they moved, she was pretty sure they were both men, although their faces were covered with black balaclavas and their baggy hoodies gave away little of their build. Seemingly unperturbed by the lights, they moved still closer to the house and she lost sight of them when they approached the back door. They both froze when they heard the back door rattle, then a thump as one of the men tried his shoulder against it. That was enough to send Agatha's security system into full frenzy, a bell sounding inside the house and a two-tone siren outside. The intruders, however, failed to reappear in the garden.

"They've gone round the front!" Agatha yelled. "That's their quickest escape route!"

She and Roy hurried through to her bedroom, where the window looked down onto her small front garden and Lilac Lane. The two men were scurrying down the path, the one with the rucksack moving awkwardly.

"Look at that one running!" Agatha shouted above the alarm's din. "He's favouring his right leg slightly— limping a bit. He's the van driver, the one whose foot I stomped on. Those are the guys who grabbed me and Toni!"

Roy nodded a brief acknowledgement but was now phoning the police. As they watched, the one with the limp paused by Agatha's car, pulling something from his rucksack. They saw a flash of flame, illuminating a bottle in his hand.

"No . . ." Agatha gasped. "He's going to . . ."

The man hurled the bottle at the car where it smashed, the fuel inside immediately blossoming into a fireball that engulfed the bonnet. Even from their vantage point behind a closed window, they could feel the surge of heat. The man took to his heels, hobbling off down the lane while the flames spread across the car, creating an inferno that lit up Lilac Lane far more effectively than its own meagre streetlights.

"Snakes and bastards!" Agatha roared. "Let's get after them!"

"No," Roy said firmly, putting an arm round her shoulders. "Toni, Simon, Patrick and Bill Wong would have my guts for garters if I let you do that . . . and so would he."

Roy pointed to James, who had appeared on his own front path, looking from the blazing car up to the bedroom window. Agatha waved to let him know they were all right.

"Not to mention Sir Charles and Mrs. Bloxby . . ." Roy continued.

"Put a sock in it, Roy," Agatha snapped. "I'll go and turn off the alarm."

With the alarm's cacophony silenced, she joined James outside, staying well back from the car.

"What on earth's going on?" James asked, the approach of distant sirens audible now the alarm had been turned off.

"Two slimebags just torched my car." Agatha sighed, unable to take her eyes off the blazing wreck. "My best make-up bag was in the glove compartment. Some of my favourite bits and pieces were in there. They're going to pay for that! When I get my hands on them, they're going to wish they'd never come anywhere near Lilac Lane! They're going to wish they'd never even heard of Agatha Raisin! They're going to wish they'd never been born!"

Chapter Six

"Blimey, Mrs. Raisin, that's a proper mess, ain't it?" The postman strolled up the path just as the last of the fire appliances trundled off down Lilac Lane. "Nobody hurt, I hope?"

"Not yet," Agatha said grimly, staring at the charred wreck of her car, thinking of the two black-clad men.

"I feel right sorry for you, Mrs. Raisin. Last time we had the fire brigade out around here it was your house," the postman said, handing Agatha her mail. "This time it's your car. That's proper bad luck, that is."

Agatha, who had dressed in a cream-coloured cashmere rollneck sweater and dark blue woollen slacks while the firemen extinguished the blaze, walked down her garden path with the postman. He'd regaled her with the tale of when his uncle had set fire to his wooden outside toilet while smoking his pipe and studying the

Racing Post, trying to pick a winner in the two-thirty at Cheltenham. He lost his list of runners and riders as well as his best trousers in the blaze.

She stood beside the twisted, burned-out shell of her car, wistfully staring at the remains of the glove compartment where her make-up bag had been. All of the cosmetics and other indispensable items that had been in there were, of course, replaceable and replicated in her bedroom, but that wasn't the point. Having a carefully chosen collection like that in the car was essential. She had always scoffed at men who thought they were being clever when they said that a woman's car was "an extension of her handbag." Total crap. It was far more important than that. The car was more like an extension of her dressing table, good light and multiple mirrors making it the best possible place for emergency make-up repairs. She thought about what the postman had said. Last time it had been her house. Two thugs sent by a gangster she was investigating had almost succeeded in burning the place down with her inside. Sometimes being Agatha Raisin, or even being near her, could be seriously bad for your health.

Bill Wong walked towards her with Margaret Bloxby at his side. Bill had been there with the first of the police officers to arrive when the car was still ablaze. Having now scoured Lilac Lane looking for any trace of the arsonists, he bumped into Margaret who was heading for Agatha's cottage. This was her second visit of the morning, having rushed round to check on Agatha when the entire village had been roused by the arrival of the police and fire brigade.

"Good morning again, Mrs. Raisin," Margaret said, with a gentle smile of empathy. "You must be exhausted after all this."

"Not really," Agatha said, shrugging. "I've drunk enough coffee to keep Brazil in business for a year and all I want to do now is to get into the office and start tracking down the rats who did this, and the pigs who murdered Mr. Tinkler, and the . . ."

"Let's go inside, Agatha," Bill said, pushing open her front gate. "We need to talk about the rats, and the pigs, and any other creatures you're dealing with."

Bill sat Agatha down in her living room, Margaret sat opposite her, and Roy and James walked through from the kitchen, each holding a mug of coffee. Agatha eyed them all suspiciously. They all had the same expression of grave concern. They had the look of a bunch with something to say—a delegation who all wanted to deliver the same message but were too lily-livered to do it on their own. Agatha felt a buzz of annoyance when she realised they had been talking about her, sneaking about behind her back while she had been watching the firefighters fail to save her make-up.

"So what's this?" Agatha said, still brandishing the sheaf of letters delivered by the postman and using it to point at each of them in a long sweep of the room.

"It's your mail," Roy said with a confused frown.

"Not this!" Agatha jumped to her feet, slapping the letters down on her coffee table. "This!" She swept a hand again to indicate the assembled quartet of guests. "This little group you've formed to pass judgement on me? I feel like I'm standing in front of a mini jury!"

"It's not like that, Agatha," Margaret said. "We're concerned about you, that's all. We simply want to—"

She stopped abruptly, her eyes having been drawn to one of the envelopes on the table—a small, square envelope neatly addressed in handwritten capital letters. Agatha followed her stare and snatched up the envelope, tearing it open. She scanned the single sheet of paper inside.

GIVE AND TAKE

YOU MAY GIVE IT BUT SHOULD NEVER WASTE IT

IF I TAKE IT I WILL NEVER HAVE IT

YOU MAY REMEMBER IT BUT NOT ALL OF IT

YOURS CAN ONLY GO ONWARDS

BUT I WILL END IT

She tutted and handed the riddle to Margaret. The others crowded round to look over Margaret's shoulder as she read the contents out loud.

"It's another death threat," James announced. "No doubt about it."

"I agree," said Bill, "although this one's more about life than death. The first line says how you can 'give it,' meaning give or devote your life to something or someone, but that you should never waste your life."

"Yes, life fits throughout," Margaret said. "The second line talks about taking a life, meaning to kill someone, but not being able to have that life, or a proper one of your own if you are locked up for murder."

"Then comes the line about remembering your life." Roy joined in. "You can remember some of it but not everything throughout your whole life."

"And the final line is the actual threat," Bill said. "Your life can only go forwards, you can't go back and relive things, but the riddler can end it by killing you."

"Agatha, my dear," said James. "This proves that those two who turned up last night intended to kill you."

"Rubbish!" Agatha argued. "It proves nothing of the sort."

"Why do you say that?" Roy asked. "The riddler says he's going to end your life!"

"That's not what the riddler wants at all," Agatha countered. "The riddler wants to tease me. For some reason he or she wants to antagonise me, frighten me and pit their wits against me. They're daring me to try to find them and having a good laugh at my expense, proving to themselves that they're smarter than I am. That all ends if I'm dead.

"Just as the shop burglaries are *not* connected to Mr. Tinkler's murder, this," she took the riddle back from Margaret and waved it in the air while pointing out the window towards the remains of her car with her free hand, "is *not* connected to *that*, and the reason is painfully obvious."

"How so?" asked James.

"Because this riddle could only have been written yesterday at the latest," Agatha explained, picking up the square envelope. "It arrived this morning in the ordinary post and the postmark shows that it was processed yesterday. There's no way it could have reached me any time before first post this morning. What point would there be in sending it if the riddler also sent those two creeps out to kill me last night? I couldn't read it if I was dead, could I? And killing me spoils the whole game—you can't scare or pit your wits against a dead person."

"The fact remains that 'those two creeps' did try to kill you last night," Roy pointed out, "and they tried to abduct you from outside your office. You are being targeted and if the men last night aren't working for the riddler, that just makes things worse."

"Roy's right," said Margaret. "You could have two different sets of thugs after you."

"I doubt it," Agatha said. "I even doubt that they were here to kill me. Why bring a homemade petrol bomb? It's not a great weapon for an assassination—not very precise. Even if they had managed to set the house on fire, Roy and I could have escaped. I survived last time somebody tried to torch the place. And if they'd intended to do that, they could simply have smashed a window and lobbed the bomb in. I don't think they were just after me. They had another motive and the petrol bomb was probably to cover their tracks—destroy evidence. It's amateur stuff, though. Too poorly planned for a professional hit or burglary. There's more to this than meets the eye."

"That may be," Bill said, "but there is still overwhelming evidence pointing to the fact that you are in danger, and that puts those around you in danger, too. Outside your office it was Toni. Here, in your own home, it was Roy. The men behind the attacks may have made mistakes but I doubt they're going to give up . . . and they only have to get lucky once to get their hands on you."

"And that's why I need to get to the office now!" Agatha snapped, her suspicions about the motive of her assembled friends setting her temper fuse fizzing. "I need to start going through old case files. If someone I've tangled with in the past is back playing games, there could be something in there that will help me find them!"

"You're absolutely the best person to find them, Agatha," Roy said, "but maybe not from the office."

"They know your office and they know your home," Margaret said. "You need to work on finding them from somewhere safe."

"Somewhere safe?" Agatha could scarcely believe her ears. "You expect me to hide? You think that I can just run away and hide somewhere?"

"Not hide, my dear," said James. "Just take them by surprise. Deploy tactics that they're not expecting. Catch them off guard—devise a different plan of attack."

"It doesn't matter how you dress it up!" Agatha roared, her fury flaring as fiery as the petrol bomb. "You all want me to turn tail and leg it! Well, I've got news for you! Agatha Raisin doesn't run away from anyone! Now get out of my house, the lot of you!"

There was an awkward silence and they all shuffled towards the front door, Roy at the end of the queue.

"Not you, Roy!" Agatha yelled. "You're living here, remember? Get your act together. We're leaving for the office in ten minutes!"

In her office, Agatha and Toni had time for a briefing from Patrick prior to leaving for their meeting with Stuart Sculley at Sculley Security Systems.

"What do I need to know before we talk to Mr. Sculley, Patrick?"

"When he set up his business here a couple of years ago," Patrick said, "Sculley Security Systems really took off and was doing well . . . until recently. At one time he had a dozen staff. Most of them have been laid off. A mate of mine who fits alarm systems for a rival company says Sculley hasn't sold a new system in more than two months."

"So things have been going badly for him since the start of the burglary epidemic," Agatha said. "That's understandable if every victim had one of his alarms. Word gets around about things like that."

"It does," Patrick agreed. "Especially given that members of the chamber of commerce have been talking to each other about the raids enough to want to bring us in to investigate . . . but according to my mate, Sculley was struggling well before the first of the raids."

"Enough for him to start robbing his clients?" Toni asked.

"Who knows, but if he's got financial problems, maybe that gives him a motive."

"Surely he would realise that he would be the prime suspect for a string of burglaries on places all fitted with his alarms?" Agatha said. "Or could that be his double bluff? He thought nobody would suspect him because he was such an obvious candidate?"

"Could be." Patrick nodded, opening a laptop and turning it so that Agatha and Toni could see the screen. "But Sculley has an alibi for every single one of the raids. He's been trying to expand his business down south in London. Bill Wong told me which hotel in Kensington he stays at and I was able to pull a few strings to get hold of some security-camera footage."

He scrolled through a series of stills showing Sculley's van arriving in the hotel's underground car park, then much clearer, moving footage of Sculley checking in at the front desk.

"The camera in the corner of the reception area shows him checking in when he said he did, then going to dinner with what must be a potential client in the hotel restaurant, handing his key to the receptionist when he goes out for a stroll, then picking up his key again before he goes up to his room for the night. He has business meetings the following day, then checks out to head home. We can then see his van leaving the hotel car park."

"Same hotel every time? Same sort of routine?"

"Exactly the same one. It seems he's a creature of habit."

"Rewind the recording to where he's picking up his key before going to bed," Agatha said. "There—that's definitely him. He looks straight up at the camera. The receptionist is chatting to him. Why isn't Sculley looking at him? Who stares at security cameras on the ceiling in the corner of the room when you're in the middle of a conversation?"

"Someone with a professional interest?" Toni suggested. "He sells and installs the things, after all."

"Or someone who wants to make sure he's seen," Patrick said.

"Exactly—someone making sure he has an alibi," Agatha agreed. "Patrick, there's bound to be a way he could have sneaked out of the hotel late at night without going through Reception. See if you can pull a few more strings and pick him up on a different camera. Toni, let's go and have a word with Mr. Sculley."

"Honestly, Mrs. Raisin, I'm at my wits' end," Stuart Sculley said, gesturing to two seats in front of his office desk. He was wearing a dark-green sweater with the stylised padlock that was his company logo on the right breast. Arched above the logo were the words "Sculley Security Systems." "These burglaries are ruining my business!"

"Your friends at the chamber of commerce are also very concerned," Agatha said, looking beyond Sculley out of the grimy window to where weeds, rusted rail tracks and wind-blown litter dominated the disused railway marshalling yards. Sculley's office was on the first floor of a small warehouse, the ground floor housing numerous boxes of equipment and racks of tools.

"I'm not surprised," Sculley said, wringing his hands. He was of slim build with short, dark hair and Agatha judged him to be in his mid-forties, although the worry lines on his face tended to make him look older. "Every single one of the raids has been on premises where I have fitted the security systems!"

"You can understand why some people have begun to think that's more than just a coincidence," Toni said.

"Of course!" Sculley said. "Obviously people are going to suspect I'm involved. In their position, I'm sure I would think exactly the same—but I'm not the one behind all this! Overall, my clients have lost goods worth over two hundred thousand pounds. Some have even threatened to sue me!"

A young woman entered the room, carrying a tray loaded with coffee cups and a plate of digestive biscuits.

"Here we are," she announced breezily. "Just as you ordered. Black for you, Stuart, and white no sugar for the ladies."

"Thank you, Yvonne," Sculley said, and while the young woman placed the coffees on the desk, Agatha looked round the room. The office was neat, but not spotlessly clean. The woodwork was painted an unimaginative shade of grey-blue and the walls might once have been white. There were two tall filing cabinets and a couple of photographs on the walls of sports cars and motorbikes, as well as several showing Sculley shaking hands with smiling customers and local celebrities.

In some of the pictures there were others wearing the green company sweater.

"How many employees do you have here, Mr. Sculley?" Agatha asked.

"We had quite a few at one time," Sculley said, bristling slightly, as though anxious not to admit just how far his business had fallen. "Now it's more convenient to hire freelance fitters and engineers when they're required."

"Did you carry out background checks on those you employed?" asked Toni.

"That didn't seem necessary at the time," Sculley explained. "Some I already knew. I used to work as an engineer myself, you see, so I was able to employ people I knew or who came recommended, all with good references."

"We carry out a lot of background checks for employers," Agatha said. "They're more thorough than simple references."

"When the police spoke to me," Sculley said, "they told me they'd be taking a look at everyone who has worked here since I set up the business."

"We will as well," Agatha informed him. "Toni will need a list of your employees."

"It's a short list at the moment." Sculley sighed. "There's just me and Yvonne. I've been spending a lot of time in London recently, though, and I'm close to a couple of big contracts there that will turn things around."

"You'll have to hope news of the burglaries doesn't scare off your new clients," Agatha said.

"That's exactly why I'm so keen for you to get to the bottom of this mess," Sculley said. "Believe me, Mrs.

Raisin, I want to find out who's behind this as much as you do—and quickly. Yvonne will supply details of everyone who's worked here. You will keep me informed of your progress, won't you?"

They chatted for a while longer about the range of security systems Sculley sold and his background in the business. When they were finished, Sculley asked again that Agatha stay in touch.

"I'm a member of the chamber, after all," he pointed out, "and, in a way, I suppose that means I'm partly your client. Whatever you find out, let me know. I may be able to help."

On their way out, Agatha and Toni stopped at Yvonne's desk in Sculley's tiny outer office. While she flicked through some files in a cabinet, promising Toni that she would scan and send to her any employee details she didn't already have on the computer, Agatha studied Yvonne. She was slim and looked fit, probably in her early thirties with dark shoulder-length hair and a pretty face. By the way she held her head in consciously cute poses, it was obvious that she enjoyed people looking at her. She enjoyed being the centre of attention, the one that people would always admire and remember. That, Agatha judged, gave Yvonne enviable self-confidence . . . or was she simply smug.

Agatha also examined Yvonne's workspace. There was a computer screen and keyboard on her desk, along with a phone, a mug full of pens and pencils, and a photograph of Yvonne wearing a ski helmet and jacket. The blue sky and snowscape background, along with a sign that read ASPEN, identified the location as one of the United States' top ski resorts. At Yvonne's side was a man wearing a ski helmet, dark, reflective goggles that obscured most of his face and a scarf that covered his chin.

"You like to ski, Yvonne?" Agatha asked.

"Love it!" the younger woman replied with a beaming smile. "Especially in the States. Mammoth Mountain, Vail, Breckenridge—the American resorts are amazing."

"Skiing is so glamorous," Toni said, seeing Agatha give a secret nod towards the photograph. "Do you go with someone?"

"I can always find a friend to come along," Yvonne replied. "During the ski season anyone who knows anything about skiing simply can't wait to get out in the mountains. I take it neither of you ski?"

"I prefer warmer pastimes," Agatha said.

"And I'm sure you can always find a friend for 'warmer pastimes,' Mrs. Raisin," Yvonne said, smiling playfully. "Now, anything else I can help you with apart from these files?"

"I don't think so," Agatha said, returning the younger woman's smile. "Goodbye, Yvonne."

They walked downstairs without saying a word, then looked at each other once they were settled in Toni's car.

"Yvonne's quite a character, isn't she?" Agatha said.

"Seems a bit full of herself to me," Toni answered. "She won't be so smart when her age starts wearing away that cutesy look."

"And at what age does a woman's beauty start wearing away?" The narrowing of Agatha's eyes gave Toni fair warning that she should choose her next words carefully.

"For a glamorous woman with style and taste," said

Toni slowly, skilfully extricating herself from a potential Raisin bear trap, "it never does."

"Good answer," Agatha said, nodding. "Yvonne appears to enjoy very expensive ski holidays."

"Not the sort of holiday you can easily afford on what she must be earning," Toni commented.

"Affordable if you have a friend paying for them," Agatha said with a wry smile, "and unless I'm very much mistaken, the friend in the photograph was Stuart Sculley."

"Not easy to identify in all that ski gear," Toni said, "but I think you're right. I bet that relationship doesn't show up on her background check."

"What did you make of Mr. Sculley?" Agatha asked.

"I'd say he was pretty upset by the burglaries," Toni replied.

"Or a very good actor," Agatha argued. "If he's taking his secretary off on luxury ski breaks, then my guess is he's burning through cash far faster than he can earn it. See what the employee background checks throw up, Toni, but, in spite of his alibi, Stuart Sculley stays top of our suspect list."

Toni started the car and headed back across Mircester towards the office.

"We do, of course, have other suspects to track down— murder suspects," Agatha said.

"It's possible they're the same two who tried to kidnap us," said Toni.

"Possible," Agatha said. "Those were certainly the ones who torched my car. We need to get a look at the pub's security camera again.

"Already on it," Toni said. "I mentioned it to Simon and he's been checking it out."

Agatha gave Toni a quizzical look and raised an eyebrow.

"I know you didn't ask us to do it, but Simon volunteered as soon as I explained what went on last night. We can get things done on our own initiative sometimes, you know."

"Yes, I do know—I've trained you well enough to know that," Agatha said, immediately taking credit for any "initiative" they had shown. "I hope you didn't tell him about—"

"The ghost of Timothy Tinkler?" Toni interrupted, sounding slightly miffed that Agatha had shown no appreciation for her and Simon's forethought. "I didn't say a thing."

"Good. Let's keep it that way for the time being."

Nothing more was said on the way back to the office and Agatha slowly realised that she had probably offended Toni by not heaping praise on her. She sighed and looked out the window as they pulled into their usual car park. What did the silly girl expect? She was doing her job just as she was supposed to, just as she was paid to do. What did she want—a medal from the king? *I don't have time for that sort of nonsense,* she told herself. *I've got the murder, the kidnap attempt, the burglaries, the extravaganza and those stupid notes to think about—too much to be pussyfooting around other people's feelings!*

By the time they reached the office the atmosphere between them, despite the increasingly mild weather, was distinctly frosty. Their arrival coincided with that of

Simon, who was triumphantly brandishing a computer flash drive.

"I got the footage, boss!" he announced. "A copy of the whole night's recording's all on here. I met the bar manager this morning when she was waiting for a delivery from the brewery and she's . . . well . . . a sort of friend, you might say . . ."

"Or I might not," Agatha said abruptly, "especially if it led the conversation anywhere near your murky love life. Let's look at it in my room. You, too, Toni."

They stood around Agatha's desk while Simon plugged the flash drive into her laptop and opened the file with the security-camera footage. He was about to press "play" when Agatha stayed his hand.

"Wait a minute," she said. "I've just realised what might be on here. Did your bar manager friend see this?"

"No," Simon said. "Nobody's looked at it. She said Bill Wong was coming to take a look this afternoon."

Agatha started the recording, which showed the front of the antiques shop from the same angle as the night Mr. Tinkler had been murdered. The image was as dark, grainy and grey as before but the street was empty. Simon fast-forwarded to where Agatha and Toni stepped out onto the pavement. Their attackers' van then appeared, obscuring the fight that ensued just before the shop lights came on.

"Looks like we miss the best bit of the show," Simon said, freezing the picture with the driver limping back to his cab. "There's better lighting here, though. We might be able to enhance that frame to get the full licence plate."

He then let the recording play again, the van racing off to reveal Agatha and Toni, recovering, then turning in horror to see the apparition appear from the shop. Simon recoiled from the screen.

"Wait, that's . . ." Simon looked from Agatha to Toni, confused, searching for an explanation. Agatha stopped the recording.

"Sit down, both of you," she said, then looked them each in the eye. "You two, along with Patrick, are the people I most trust, and can best rely on in the whole world. You did good work in getting this recording, but no one else must see it."

She explained to Simon about Tristan Tinkler and the need to keep him under wraps.

"If the police, especially Wilkes, see Tristan on that recording, we lose our surprise," Agatha said. "There's no way we can keep him a secret if anyone else knows. Wilkes will take great delight in telling all his slimy pals at his golf club about how scared we looked when we saw the 'ghost.'"

"Can you get back in there, Simon?" Toni asked. "Maybe sabotage the original recording?"

"No worries," Simon said. "I'll get over there now and tell the manager that I messed up the file transfer. I can go back into their system and delete everything from the moment the van drives off. To anyone who looks at the file after that, it will look like I made another balls-up."

"Good," Agatha said, and looked straight at Toni. "I might not always make it obvious, but I really do appreciate all the hard work you two do."

"Thanks, boss," Simon said. "I'll get going now."

Toni looked down at the laptop, then back at Agatha, smiled and nodded. Not for the first time, Agatha reminded herself that a few carefully chosen words could help avoid any amount of pussyfooting.

Agatha had been working at her desk for an hour or so and was beginning to think about lunch when her phone rang. It was Martin Randall.

"I wanted to let you know how sorry I am about your friend, Timothy Tinkler," Randall said. "That was a terrible thing for you to go through."

"Rest assured I will find who did it, Mr. Randall."

"Please, you must call me Martin, and . . . I know this might sound awkward at a time like this, but . . . might you be free for dinner this evening?"

Agatha was about to turn him down, then paused for a moment. She had lost a lot of sleep the previous night and had been looking forward to a quiet evening at home, yet Martin Randall was a contact she needed to cultivate and the extravaganza was drawing closer by the day. He also seemed quite charming and was very easy on the eye . . .

"An early dinner would be a lovely idea, Martin," she said. "I don't think I can stay out too late after all that happened last night."

"Last night? Sounds like you live a very exciting life, Agatha."

Agatha promised to explain everything later and they agreed to meet at an Italian restaurant they both knew not far from her office. By the time her phone clicked off she had opened the drawer in her desk where she kept her office make-up stash. Ordinarily, she would have rushed home before a date with a man like Martin Randall, but her car was gone, and her car's vital cosmetics bag was gone. The desk-drawer alternative, combined with what was in her handbag, looked sufficient, but the sweater she was wearing could not go to dinner, even in a Mircester Italian. Fortunately, she'd spotted a top that would be ideal in a high-street boutique window the previous week, so she dealt with this emergency like she had with so many in the past. When the going gets tough, the tough go shopping!

"Rolex, Cartier, Longines, Tiffany, Breitling," Agatha read through the list with mounting amazement. "There are some seriously posh watches and jewellery here, Roy."

Agatha handed the list of items that had been donated for auction at the extravaganza back across her desk to Roy, who looked excessively pleased with himself.

"I asked a few of our sponsors to donate, Charles said Gustav made a few 'persuasive' calls and Mrs. Tassy strong-armed the rest," Roy said.

"I can well imagine the tactics those two were able to use," Agatha said, laughing. "All this in just a couple of days . . ."

"Paintings and furniture have been pledged, too," Roy promised, "but I thought the sparkly things would be best to make a start on a catalogue."

"Ah, yes, the catalogue," Agatha said. "I'll be talking

to Martin Randall about that this evening, so you'll have to make your own plans for dinner."

"Ooooh . . . he's a fast mover, isn't he?"

"It's a business dinner, Roy, nothing more."

"So you say now, sweetie, but in the heat of the moment . . . well, you know what I mean. Just you be careful and don't do anything I wouldn't do."

"Well, that leaves me plenty of scope, doesn't it?"

Roy stood to leave and Toni, who had been hovering outside, took her chance to grab some of her boss's time.

"Simon has doctored the security footage," she said as soon as the door was closed, "so the secret is safe, but I still don't see how the 'ghost' thing is going to work for us."

"Neither do I just yet," Agatha said, "but as long as he's a secret, we can bring Tristan into play when we eventually need him."

"How are you feeling now, after all that stuff last night?"

"I'm fine. I got off lightly. All I lost was a dressing table."

"It was your car that was set alight."

"Car, dressing table, whatever . . ." Agatha yawned and stretched.

"You must be tired," Toni said.

"A bit. It's been an exhausting couple of days. On top of everything, I had what felt like a mutiny in my living room this morning," Agatha explained. "People I thought were on my side were suddenly ganging up against me."

"Yeah, I heard about that," Toni said, and laughed.

"Bill Wong phoned sounding a bit sheepish. He said they'd tried to get you to lie low and that you'd gone a bit 'Raisin' on them. Sometimes I think they don't know you at all!"

"I suppose they thought they were doing the right thing," Agatha said with a sigh. "You don't think I should run away somewhere, do you?"

"Not a bit. You've got too much work to do."

"Precisely—and now I need to start delving into old cases as well."

"On the other hand," Toni said, holding up her mobile phone, "you have one of these that will keep you in touch with me, Roy, Charles or anybody else you need to talk to from anywhere you like. You also have one of these," she tapped Agatha's laptop, "which can be loaded with every case file we've got as well as sending and receiving emails from anywhere in the world. On top of that, you have airline tickets for a flight to Mallorca that leaves tomorrow afternoon, where you have your very own, ex-police, dancing bodyguard to keep an eye on you . . ."

"You've been recruited by the mutineers, haven't you?"

"No. You can always count on me. I'm on your side, whatever you choose to do, *always*."

"Thank you, Toni. I know . . ."

She was interrupted by a roaring, angry voice and footsteps booming across the outer office so violently they made the door shudder.

"Where is she? Where is that damn woman?"

Agatha and Toni stepped out of her room into the

main office to see DCI Wilkes standing in the middle of the floor, his greasy dark hair in disarray from having run up the stairs, half his front shirt tail untucked and with one pocket of his brown suit having turned itself inside out with excitement. His face was crimson.

Agatha took in the scene with a glance. Patrick was out, Simon had stood to intercept Wilkes but plucky Helen Freedman, a middle-aged woman in glasses who barely came up to the lanky Wilkes's chest, had beaten him to it. She stood resolutely in front of the furious Wilkes, barring his way to Agatha's office.

"How dare you come barging into this office!" Helen scolded him, shaking her fist. "You calm down and stay right where you are or I'll give you a punch in the nose, young man!"

"Then I'll have you for assaulting a police officer, just like I'm going to have your boss!" Wilkes snarled, baring his teeth.

"It's all right, Helen," Agatha said. "You can leave this to me."

"Agatha Raisin!" Wilkes growled. "Just the woman I've been looking for."

"You flatter me," Agatha replied. "I'm sure you've been looking for a woman for years."

Wilkes sneered. "You think you're so clever, but I know how to handle women like you."

"I very much doubt that," Agatha said. "You know even less about women than you do about choosing a suit. I bet the last woman to hold your hand was checking for a pulse, although I doubt she found one on a zombie like you."

"What happened to the police tape securing my crime scene downstairs?" Wilkes yelled.

"I can assure you, I didn't touch it."

"And what happened to the security-camera recordings from the King Charles? I hear your office boy over there was tampering with them—tampering with evidence is a serious offence."

"I've seen the recording," Agatha assured him, "and what it shows is evidence of the crime that was committed last night—the assault on myself and Miss Gilmour. Accidents happen when it comes to technology but, in any case, you can't prove there was anything else on that recording pertinent to any crime."

"Don't underestimate me, Mrs. Raisin!"

"Even I can't do the impossible. Now I must ask you to leave. I'm really rather busy this afternoon, so maybe I can ignore you some other time?"

"I want any recordings you've got from the King Charles cameras!" Wilkes held out his hand.

"Unless you have a search warrant, you're leaving with that hand just as empty as it is now. Good afternoon, DCI Wilkes."

"I'll be back!" Wilkes shouted, waving a finger at Agatha before turning on his heel and marching off down the stairs.

"Simon," Agatha said, once Wilkes had gone. "Do you have a flash drive with the film of the van but the last part deleted?"

"Yes, boss," Simon said. "Just as it now is on the pub system."

"If Wilkes, or any other cop he sends, asks for our

footage when I'm not here, you give him that version, okay? Let me have the original version."

Simon handed her the flash drive and she closed her fingers around it, staring at her clenched fist.

"What are you going to do now?" Toni asked.

"I'm going to get changed and go out to dinner," Agatha replied with a smile. "Then I might just leave the country!"

Chapter Seven

As a high-flying PR executive in London, Agatha had dined at some of the finest restaurants in the city and had a keen appreciation of the gastronomic delights talented chefs could produce. In the Cotswolds, she had sampled the area's most prestigious restaurants, in the past most often in the company of Charles who, during his worst periods of financial trauma, had regularly "absent-mindedly" left his wallet on his desk at Barfield House. The Feathers gastropub in Carsely's neighbouring village, Ancombe, was one of her favourites for excellent, if expensive, food. The Red Lion pub in Carsely itself offered a more affordable, if less sophisticated menu, but she still enjoyed chipping the tasty, crusty bits of lasagne off the dish that the pub's chef had baked on with a lack of finesse that was still a cut above her own microwaved efforts.

The Cotswolds, therefore, offered a wide range of restaurants Agatha enjoyed and even downtrodden Mircester boasted a handful. Casa Giulia was one of them. The restaurant was in a small side street on the other side of Mircester High Street from the lane where Agatha's office was. The entrance looked like a small shopfront, its frosted window etched with the restaurant's name and its woodwork painted a dark, glossy red. Martin Randall was waiting by the window when Agatha arrived, smiling and waving as she walked round the corner from the high street.

"Agatha, how lovely to see you again!" He greeted her with another beaming smile, a warm handshake and then, after a short, almost awkward pause, a polite peck on the cheek. "How are you? No, don't answer that, let's just get inside and order a bottle of their delicious sagrantino, then we can talk properly."

Inside, the restaurant opened out like a secret cavern, softly lit and with enough tables to make it seem popular, but not so many as to make it overcrowded. The walls were decorated with photographs ancient and modern showing the hilltop towns, forests, valleys and lakes of Umbria. Having eaten in Casa Giulia before, Agatha had almost decided what she was going to have before leaving her office and chatted with Randall about their separate travels through Italy while the waiter poured the wine and they perused the menu. She was torn between the two dishes she had tried before—*colombaccio,* spit-roasted wood pigeon, or *pasta alla Norcina*, a creamy sauce loaded with Umbrian mushrooms and wild boar sausage meat served with a kind of square spaghetti called strangozzi. She opted for the pasta.

"So how are you doing with that lovely old clock?" Randall asked after they clinked glasses of the dark red wine. "A friend spotted it in Timothy Tinkler's shop window, but it's gone now. Got someone working on it for you?"

"To be honest," Agatha answered, without being entirely honest, "I haven't had much time to think about that with everything else that's been happening."

She explained about the attempted abduction and the car fire.

"But that's dreadful!" Randall seemed genuinely shocked, leaving Agatha a little surprised that he had heard nothing about the fire either through the grapevine or on local radio news. If she knew Carsely, then everyone would have been talking about the firebombing of her car, and the gossip would certainly have spread to Mircester during the course of the day. Maybe listening to tittle-tattle was beneath Randall, although that hardly seemed likely given the string of questions that followed.

"Who would try to break in and then set your car on fire?" he wondered, looking appalled at the thought. "They should be locked up! I bet you're already on their trail, aren't you?"

"We'll find them sooner or later," Agatha said. "I won't give up until we do."

"But do you have any leads you're following?" Randall asked. "Have they been careless enough to leave you anything to work with?"

"We heard this afternoon that the police found the van the two men used abandoned on the outskirts of town," Agatha said, slightly wary of Randall's questions. His probing felt like it was going beyond polite interest. "There were so many different prints on it that it could take weeks to sort them all out, and even then there's no guarantee that any of them belonged to the two who attacked us. They were wearing gloves."

"Disappointing," Randall said, nodding. "Have you anything else to go on?"

"My team's looking into it. We'll get them, you can be sure of that."

"I was surprised your clock turned up in the antiques shop window," Randall said, returning to his original topic. "It's a lovely object, but it wasn't actually working . . . unless you had someone fix it?"

"I think Mr. Tinkler simply thought it would look nice on display," Agatha said, noting Randall's persistent interest in the clock. Was he again showing a little more than a casual interest, or was that just her naturally suspicious nature? "I might put it back there for a while once it's running—a sort of tribute to him."

"That's a nice idea," Randall agreed, "providing whoever eventually takes over the shop agrees. I can help find someone to repair the clock, if you like."

"I'd rather not think about that right now," Agatha said, deciding to terminate the clock conversation without letting Randall press her further, "but there is something that I would like your help with."

She explained about the Great Barfield Extravaganza as the waiter brought their food. She described how it was all coming together as an upmarket, invitation-only event full of fun, colour and excitement with everything from fairground attractions and balloon rides to a fashion show . . . and a charity auction.

"I think you can guess which bit I'd like your help with," she said, smiling and sampling her wine.

"Charity events are all very well . . ." Randall said, hesitating, pushing some of his pappardelle pasta around in its hare and bacon sauce, "but if I'm to be involved, the reputation of my business demands that I do everything as Randall Auctions is expected to do. That means producing a proper catalogue, for one thing, and I doubt even that can be done in time."

"Eleanor Roosevelt once said that 'Nothing has ever been achieved by the person who says it can't be done,'" Agatha said, producing from her handbag a list of items already pledged. She slid it across the table to him. "This is just the start. We will have much more confirmed over the next few days."

"I see . . ." Randall said, scanning the list with an appraising eye. "Nevertheless, to organise everything as I would want in the time you have available would mean diverting significant resources from my company and we . . ."

Agatha handed him another sheet of paper, this one filled with names.

"These are just some of the people who are donating items and will be in attendance on the day," she said, watching Randall register each titled aristocrat, business high-flyer and captain of industry on the list. "Some of these people I'm sure you already know. Others are people you really should have in your contacts book. Can you really afford to let them see some other auctioneer running our show?"

"I do get your point, but . . ."

"And you know these people will overbid on our already very expensive auction lots." Agatha sensed he was weakening and went in for the kill. "They'll want to be seen to be doing their bit for charity. As I understand it, the auctioneer's fee is usually a percentage of the sale price of an item. Those spectacularly high prices will generate large fees and while the proceeds from the sales will go to good causes, there's no reason why you shouldn't be compensated in the usual way for your time, effort and expenses."

"Very well," Randall said, clinking glasses with Agatha to seal the deal. "I'll do it! I'm very lucky to be having dinner with a glamorous woman of taste who also understands business!"

"Oh, I'm much more than that, Martin," Agatha replied, doing her best to tone a triumphant grin down to a more demure smile.

"I bet you are. You know, we're going to be seeing a lot more of each other in the near future. Why don't we start by going on from here to—"

Agatha held up a hand, signalling him to stop, but continuing to smile to let him know she appreciated what he was about to say.

"Not tonight, I'm afraid," she said. "Let's just enjoy the rest of this excellent food before I have to head home. I'm tired and I've got another busy day ahead tomorrow."

He nodded and returned to his pasta, the conversation settling into tales of past adventures in Italy and Agatha's Eleanor Roosevelt quote prompting a discussion about powerful women they both admired. Randall did not mention either the two men in black who had attacked her or the clock again, but even as she stepped into the taxi taking her home to Carsely, an uncomfortable suspicion nagged at Agatha. Martin Randall was a good-looking, charming man who clearly wanted to make theirs more than just a business relationship, yet she didn't quite trust him. He wasn't like John. He didn't have John's dependable strength and gentle nature. John—she missed him. She sat bolt upright in the back of the taxi.

"I need to turn this around!" she said, then held a hand over her mouth, realising that what she was thinking had burst its way out.

"Have I gone the wrong way, miss?" asked the driver.

"No, you're fine," she said. "I was just thinking out loud."

She wasn't going to let the murderers, the kidnappers, the burglars and the riddler stop her from doing what she wanted to do, and what she really wanted to do was fly out to be with John! She wasn't running away from them—she would go to Mallorca because that's where *she* wanted to be! She wanted to be on board the *Ocean Palace Splendour* with John. He would listen to everything she had to say and help her sort it all out. She could rely on him. She could trust him. Then, once she'd had some breathing space to get everything straight in her head, all those creeps dressed in black had best watch out!

"You don't have to worry about a thing on the extravaganza, sweetie," Roy said, attempting to lift Agatha's suitcase, feeling the weight and then leaving it for Charles. "The whole schedule for the day is falling into place very nicely. Now that we've set the ball rolling, all I need to do is to keep on top of things and keep pushing people to do what they've said they'll do."

"I will check in with you regularly," Agatha said, tucking her mobile phone into her handbag, "but you can easily reach me if there are any problems."

"I've loaded a huge batch of case files onto your laptop," Toni said. She had arrived at Agatha's cottage around the same time as Charles, who had insisted on driving Agatha to the airport. James had joined them from next door to see Agatha off. They all now crowded into her hallway, with Charles about to manhandle the large suitcase out the front door.

"If there are any files you need that I haven't included, just let me know," Toni said. "I'll be talking to Bill every day, so I can update you on anything the police come up with on the murder or the burglaries."

"Tell him again not to waste time on those nonsense riddles," Agatha said. "In fact, I'll tell him myself. It has wheels, Charles." She pointed to the suitcase. He stood it upright, extended the handle and wheeled it down the path, a Knight of the Realm, the Master of Barfield

House looking a little puzzled at having just been treated like . . . a servant.

"I'll keep an eye on the house and feed the cats," James promised. "Don't worry about a thing here, my dear." Then his travel writer's instincts took over. "Take some time to check out the cathedral in Palma. It looks like a fortress from the outside, but it's glorious inside. There are also lots of Gaudí buildings hidden away in—"

"James, this isn't exactly a sightseeing tour," she said before giving him a brief hug and, after checking that her suitcase was actually loaded into the car, climbing into the Range Rover's passenger seat. Roy turned to Toni, watching Charles's car trundle down Lilac Lane.

"It seems strange already without her here," he said. "Almost as if we've been let off the hook. When the cat's away, the mice will play, sort of thing."

"We've all got too much to do to relax," Toni pointed out, giving Roy a stern warning. "Patrick, Simon and I are talking to every contact we have in order to track down Mr. Tinkler's killers and we're all pulling night-shifts to patrol the 'at risk' businesses. You've got your work cut out for you as well, remember."

"I know," Roy said defensively. "It was just a feeling . . ."

"Well, my feeling," James said, "is that if any of the mice start playing around, the cat will sense it from across the continent and be back here like a shot."

"You're right, of course," Roy said, laughing and

checking his watch. "Back to work, then. I have an appointment in less than half an hour."

Charles headed out towards Evesham but turned off for Childswickham and on to Hinton Cross before taking the A46 towards Tewkesbury and finally joining the M5 motorway all the way to Bristol.

"We'll be there in plenty of time," Charles said. "The whole journey is well under two hours—much quicker than going down to Gatwick."

"That's what I thought when I booked my flights," Agatha agreed. "I planned on driving myself then, of course . . ." She clenched her teeth and shook her head, the thought of the incinerated make-up bag still riling her. "Gatwick is more than two hours, just a bit longer than driving to London."

"Yes, providing you don't have any snarl-ups along the way," Charles said. "You can leave our neck of the woods early in the morning and be in London for breakfast."

"You can nowadays . . ." Agatha mused. "How long would it have taken William Harrison to get to London?"

"More than two days as opposed to two hours, I should think," Charles said. "The railways didn't come along until the middle of the nineteenth century and the roads weren't great, even for someone attempting the journey on horseback. Why do you want to know that?"

"Just curious," she replied, reaching for the button to recline her leather seat a little more, relaxing into

151

its cushioned splendour. "Travelling is so much easier these days, isn't it?"

"Of course." Charles glanced over to see her stretching her legs. "I could come with you, you know . . . just to keep you company."

"I'll have John there, remember?" Agatha said, closing her eyes.

"He'll be busy with other things some of the time," Charles pointed out. "I could check into a hotel and wander round Palma with you from time to time."

"Three's a crowd, Charles." Agatha sighed. "Besides, the ship's only in port for a couple of days before we sail for Tangiers, then Casablanca and Madeira."

"How long are you planning staying on board?"

"As long as I like. The more chance I get to think, the more answers I'll come up with."

Once she was on board the aircraft bound for Mallorca, having browsed designer cosmetics and jewellery in the airport's duty-free stores, Agatha considered it a decent hour to have a gin and tonic. She sipped it while reading through the glossy magazine she'd picked up at a newsstand, marvelling at scandalous intimate details from the lives of celebrities she'd never heard of. During a flight of just under two-and-a-half hours, she'd picked out at least six cases ranging from paternity disputes to property fraud where the people exposed in the magazine really needed help from Raisin Investigations.

Following a smooth landing, the aircraft taxied swiftly to the terminal where she queued to disembark and, on reaching the door, was pleasantly surprised to find that stepping out of the air-conditioned interior into the open air was not quite as dramatic an experience as she had expected. Unlike in the height of summer, the temperature in the Mallorcan sunshine was pleasantly warm rather than oppressively furnacelike. She would make it to the port to meet John without turning into a sweaty blob after all.

Once through passport control, she collected her suitcase, wheeling it through customs and out of the terminal building, where she quickly found a taxi. On the way to the port where the *Ocean Palace Splendour* was docked, she marvelled at how quick her journey had been. From sitting in Charles's car to sitting in the taxi had taken less than an afternoon, whereas she knew (because James had told her that morning) that on a seventeenth-century sailing ship, William Harrison would have taken up to three weeks to make the same journey. Why was that old story still bugging her so much, despite everything else that was going on? Was it simply the horrible miscarriage of justice—three people put to death by mistake? No, there was far more to it than that. There was something truly sinister about the Harrison mystery, and she knew that, when her cauldron of thoughts stopped bubbling quite so much, the solution to the Campden Wonder would float to the surface.

She reached for her handbag and plucked out her compact mirror and lipstick when Palma Cathedral came into view on her right. The cathedral was not, as James had said, like a fortress. It was stunning, standing proudly by the shore against a clear blue sky, the golden stone of its many spires and pinnacles rejoicing in the sunshine. Checking her make-up, however, had no religious significance. It had far more to do with the edifice that now dominated the view to her left. There, just across the Bay of Palma, lay the city's port, its buildings as well as the hotels, office and apartment blocks in the vicinity of the port dwarfed by the enormous structure that was the *Ocean Palace Splendour*. Somewhere on board, John would be waiting. That definitely warranted a quick image review.

Judging her make-up to pass muster, Agatha tidied her refurbishing tools back into her handbag and watched the gigantic ship loom ever larger in the car window. She had tried to count the decks once before, but had quickly lost interest when the vivid slashes of blue and orange paint on the superstructure had thrown her off track. The colour scheme, designed, she believed, to give the ship the look of a party venue, was, like most things that screamed "good times are happening here," really rather vulgar. She had seen the ship before and even spent the night aboard with John when it was docked at the Rome Cruise Terminal in Civitavecchia, but this time she'd be spending a lot longer aboard—a lot longer with John.

By the time the taxi driver dropped her at the terminal check-in, Agatha was feeling distinctly out of sorts. At first, she thought it might have been the coronation chicken sandwich she'd had at Bristol Airport while waiting for her flight, but, no . . . she didn't feel off colour . . . not ill exactly . . . but . . . . Then she saw her hand shaking when she went to grip the extended handle of her case and realised what was wrong. She was nervous. She was excited. She had butterflies in her tummy . . . all because she was about to see John again. *Get a grip of yourself, woman!* she told herself fiercely, then looked round to make sure she hadn't spouted it out loud. *You're acting like a flighty schoolgirl meeting her first crush! You're too old . . . no . . . too dignified for all this nonsense.*

She decided to visit the ladies' to calm herself down. Her suitcase wheels rumbled across the tiled floor and in through the door, where she was faced with a bank of mirrors and hand basins. Setting the case to rest, she examined herself in the mirror. Her make-up was still good. The light yellow dress with a subtle floral pattern had survived the journey well without creasing too much. The low, scooped neck had made it a little too chilly for England and for the air conditioning on the flight, but her pale-blue pashmina, now stowed safely in her suitcase, had compensated for that. She adjusted the small gold pendant hanging low around her neck. It had a geometric design that made her think of sails, so it had seemed appropriate for joining a ship, and still did. She then tweaked the wide brim of her white sun hat, which had endured the journey from Bristol in its own overhead locker, one withering look from Agatha having despatched the middle-aged man intent on shoving a carrier bag full of duty-free vodka in beside it.

Holding both hands level with her breasts, palms down, she slowly pushed down towards her waist while breathing out, calming herself and the butterflies.

"He lucky man," came a voice and Agatha looked to her right, startled to find a young cleaning woman standing with one hand on a mop handle and the other on her hip. She had bright, dark eyes and an infectious smile showing admirably white teeth untainted by the cigarette smoke and coffee that had resulted in Agatha lining her dentist's pocket so lavishly.

"Who is?" Agatha asked.

"Whatever man you go to see, *señora.*" The young woman smiled. "You looking *muy bien*—real good. Lucky man."

"Thank you ... um ... *gracias,*" Agatha said, then fished in her handbag to leave a ten-euro tip on the surface by the basin.

I am looking "muy bien," Agatha thought to herself, marching boldly out of the building onto the quayside, gripping the extended handle of her case, the bag following on behind her like a loyal pet. *I am Agatha Raisin and I have nothing to worry about.* She walked out along the quay towards the cruise ship that stood in the water like a gaudy graffiti mountain. Canvas-covered gangways reached out from the hull, providing easy passage from dry land to the ship's embarkation deck. Beside one of these tented bridges, among small groups of other passengers and crew, stood John, tall and handsome in a white uniform and cap. He grinned and waved when he spotted her, rushing to greet her.

"You look fantastic!" he said, his hands on her shoulders. He stooped to kiss her and she returned his kiss before placing a hand on his chest to push him away.

"You look pretty good yourself, Admiral," she said, laughing and brushing imaginary dust off his uniform shirt.

156

"The uniform's a bit silly. I haven't worn anything like this since I was a boy in the sea cadets at school. The cruise line likes to make all the senior staff look like officers," he said, laughing, then went to kiss her again. She backed away. "I know," he whispered, grinning. "Too much public affection is undignified and really only for teenagers!"

"Quite right," she said, then threw her arms around him. He lifted her off her feet and spun her around.

"Come on," he said, picking up her case. "Let's get aboard and you can see our new cabin!"

"John," she said, pointing to the extended handle. "It has wheels."

He shrugged, set the case down and towed it towards the nearest gangway, holding out his free arm for her to link in. When they stepped onto the gangway, he collapsed the suitcase handle and carried it into a carpeted elevator that whisked them up to one of the topmost decks.

"The crew don't get private balconies," he said, turning left out of the elevator, "but our cabin is right on this promenade deck, which is almost as good."

She followed him a few paces along the deck to where he stopped outside a wooden cabin door, fishing in his pocket for his key. At that moment the door to the adjacent cabin swung slowly open. A woman whom Agatha, had she been pressed to do so, could only have described as stunning stepped out onto the deck.

She was in her mid-thirties. Her hair was long, almost down to her waist, sleek and dark. Her eyes were a dazzling blue and she had cheekbones so beautifully sculpted that a tear, should she ever have reason to shed one, would surely plummet straight to earth without sullying any other part of her face. She was tall, although not as tall as John, and had the build of an athlete, lithe and slim with a flat stomach that denied she had ever suffered from the kind of late-night chocolate-brownie-and-ice-cream frenzy that, in Agatha's opinion, most normal women experienced from time to time.

Her enviable figure and lightly tanned skin were clearly evident due to the fact that the black-and-gold silk robe she was wearing had billowed open in what Agatha judged to be an entirely deliberate manner, revealing the matching black-and-gold bikini beneath.

"Johnny," she cooed, displaying a perfect smile. "I wondered where you'd got to!"

A single step took her to John's side where she slipped an arm through his, just where Agatha's arm had been only moments before, and planted a light kiss on his cheek, leaving a lipstick mark that matched the reddening of his face.

"I was just going up to our favourite spot to catch the last of the sun," she said. "Aren't you going to join me for a final breath of air before showtime?"

"Well, no, not today, I have . . ." John held out a hand to indicate Agatha's presence and eased the woman's arm out from under his own.

"You have company?" The woman sounded surprised. "Now, Johnny, I hope you haven't been fraternising with the passengers—that's strictly against the rules."

"No," John said quickly. "This is Agatha . . ."

"Oh, *you're* Agatha," the woman said. "I must say, from the way Johnny described you I thought you would be far . . ." She paused as if considering her words. "Well, nice to meet you anyway. I'm off to grab that sun. See you later, Johnny." She reached out to wipe the lipstick trace from his cheek, let her hand linger a little too long on his face, gave him a wink and wafted off round the corner.

"Who the hell was that?" Agatha demanded.

"That was my . . . um . . . new dance partner, Letitia."

"Letitia?" Agatha suddenly realised that her fists were clenched and she was standing with her back ramrod straight. "Your dance partner? You didn't mention her in any of your texts or phone calls. She seemed very *familiar* with you."

"Well, you know how it is with dance partners. You have to be good friends."

"Oh, do you?" Agatha's temper had now reached boiling point.

"Yes . . . of course. Some of the Latin and ballroom holds are quite close . . . quite intimate . . . and . . ."

"Intimate!" Agatha yelled. "Yes, I can see she was intimate all right, *Johnny*! I travelled a thousand miles and left all sorts of trouble brewing at home to be here with you and the first thing I see when I get here is you with your *intimate* good friend!"

"Listen, I can explain . . ."

"This is going to be good!"

"Well, when two people are . . . you know . . . dancing together every day, you come to see quite a lot of each other . . ."

"Your Letitia seems very happy for people to see quite a lot of her!"

". . . and there has to be a certain . . . chemistry, I suppose, and things happen, and . . ."

159

"Enough! I was wrong! It's not good—it's shit!"

"Just listen to me, will you?"

"I've heard enough! Letitia missed a bit of lipstick there—let me wipe that for you!"

She drew back an open hand and slapped his face with a sound like an afternoon thunderclap.

"I'm leaving! Don't come running after me—I never want to see you again!"

She snatched up her suitcase, struggling to balance its weight against her handbag and the carry-on bag in her other hand.

"Wait, Agatha," he pleaded with her, stepping forward to offer help. "You can't carry that . . ."

"I know!" she screeched, slamming the case down and yanking out the handle. "It has WHEELS!"

The elevator journey down to the embarkation deck was mercifully swift and Agatha was quickly striding out along the quay to where she could see a taxi loitering. As she approached, the driver stepped out—the same one who had brought her to the docks.

"A short cruise, *señora*," he said, loading her bags into the back of the car.

"Not short enough for me," Agatha said grimly.

"Where to?" the driver asked once she was in the car.

"As far away from that thing as I can get," she answered, jerking a thumb over her shoulder at the cruise liner.

"Shanghai?" suggested the driver.

"You're funny," Agatha said, without cracking a smile. "Far away on the island."

"Pollensa, maybe?"

"Perfect."

"Is expensive . . ."

"Do I look like I care? Just drive!"

The driver took her out of the port onto the coast road and past Palma Cathedral once more. Agatha stared out of the window, watching the city turn to countryside and the craggy peaks of the Serra de Tramuntana casting long shadows in the early evening light. The journey across the island from Palma in the southwest to Puerto Pollensa on the northeast coast took less than an hour, although daylight was starting to fade by the time the taxi reached the outskirts of Alcúdia, where they turned left onto the road that ran round the picturesque Bay of Pollensa to the harbour town.

"Where you like to go in Pollensa?" asked the driver, the first words that had passed between them since leaving Palma.

"Hotel Illa d'Or," Agatha answered.

"You have stayed there before, *señora*?"

"Never."

"Maybe they have no rooms tonight."

"They'll have one for me."

The driver took her round the town on a modern ring road, then into a narrow backstreet, eventually pulling up outside a grand entrance that looked like a Spanish-styled pagoda. He unloaded the bags and Agatha paid him using the last of her cash, adding a generous tip.

"I am Miguel," he said, handing her a card and circling a phone number with a stubby pencil. "I live close. You need me, I come."

Agatha thanked him and made her way through the pagoda entrance to find a stylish, modern reception area. A young man in a white shirt and blue tie greeted her pleasantly in perfect English.

"Do you have a reservation, madam?" he asked.

"No, this is a . . . spur-of-the-moment thing . . ."

"We have very few rooms available, madam, but . . ."

"I want the best you have," she said, placing a credit card on the desk that she knew would leave the receptionist in no doubt that she could afford the best. He seemed completely unfazed by the card.

"Of course, madam. One moment, please, while I check." His fingers drifted across the computer keyboard in front of him and he studied the screen for an instant. "We have a suite with a terrace that has a wonderful view out across the bay."

"I'll take it."

"How long will you be staying with us, madam?"

"I'm . . . I'm not sure."

"Not to worry. We can discuss that tomorrow, if you wish."

Once she had checked in, a young woman appeared to show Agatha up to her suite, another young man following immediately behind with her bags. The young woman opened the door for Agatha, then gave her a guided tour of the suite. There was a spacious sitting room, comfortably furnished, with light-coloured wooden floorboards polished as smooth as glass. The wood theme was used as a panel motif on the white walls and carried through to the bedroom where there was an opulent four-poster bed, yet still space for another sofa, a couple of armchairs and a coffee table. There was a large, luxuriously appointed bathroom, and two sets of glass doors led out from the bedroom onto the terrace. Standing at the carved stone balustrade, Agatha could see out past the hotel's waterside bar and restaurant to where boats and yachts of all shapes and sizes bobbed at their moorings, then on across the bay where the sun was now setting behind distant hills.

The staff left her to settle in and she found the minibar beneath the desk in the sitting room. She made herself a gin and tonic, then strolled out onto the terrace. This side of the building, rather than the grand entrance accessible by car, was clearly the public face of the Illa d'Or. She gazed out over the water. A mellow orange glow marked where the sun was dragging the daylight down behind the hills. Somewhere out there, to the south and west, John was aboard the *Ocean Palace Splendour* . . . with that woman.

Turning her back on the bay, she walked inside and looked around her bedroom. Here she was, a girl brought up in a Birmingham tower block, who had left her abusive parents when she was just a teenager and worked insanely hard to establish herself in the PR world, building her own hugely successful business. She'd then moved on to create a second business as an investigator and had sent some of the most dangerous killers in the country to jail. Here she now was, on a beautiful island in the most magnificent hotel, in a fabulous suite . . . alone.

Placing her untouched drink carefully on the coffee table, she sank slowly to her knees on the wooden floor, buried her face in her hands and cried until her sides ached.

Chapter Eight

The following morning, Agatha was woken by the sun streaming in through the terrace doors. She was lying on the four-poster, on top of the sheets. Rolling over, she tugged at her clothes. She was still wearing the yellow floral-print dress she'd been wearing the day before. According to her watch, it was just 6:30 a.m., but she knew she hadn't yet changed it to local time, most of the rest of Europe being one hour ahead of the UK. Dragging herself to the edge of the huge bed, she stood up, stretched and caught sight of herself in the mirror.

Her hair was a mess, her make-up was all over her face and her dress looked like a crumpled, lopsided paper bag—lopsided because the hem on the right had somehow managed to tuck itself into her knickers. She had a headache, but surely she hadn't . . . She looked over at the coffee table where her gin and tonic still stood, untouched. She'd had nothing to drink. The headache was from dehydration and crying. Had she really cried herself to sleep? Of course she had. The humiliation had been suffocating. The thought of going back to Carsely knowing that everyone would be talking about how she had been jilted for a . . . performing stick insect was still too much to bear. She couldn't go home yet. She needed to take stock and gather her strength. She took a bottle of water from the minibar and all but drained it, immediately feeling much better, and ravenously hungry.

"You're a mess," she told herself, returning to the mirror. "Strength gathering starts now. Get in the shower, sort yourself out and get downstairs for breakfast."

She paused for a second, taking another long look in the mirror. This was not who she wanted to be. No one would ever see her looking like this. This was not her. She was too proud and too tough to go to pieces over any man, even John Glass. He could have his skinny dancer—she had more important things to think about.

Two hours later, she was sitting under a shade on the hotel terrace restaurant by the waterfront having enjoyed a delicious continental breakfast of cold meats, cheese, bread, fruit and several cups of coffee, delivered by attentive, friendly waiters. Eating outside in the fresh air with the gentlest of breezes whispering in off the water made it all taste even better. It was also hugely refreshing that neither the hotel staff nor any of the other guests knew either who she was or anything about what was going on in her life. Here she could be anonymous and sort out her problems for herself.

The sun was now warming the bay, flooding the

whole area with light that danced on the water, creating a glare that made sunglasses a necessity when looking out over the moored boats towards Puerto Pollensa.

Agatha picked her phone up off her breakfast table. She had several missed calls, most from John, one from James, a couple from Toni, even one from Margaret. There were voice messages from the same. She dismissed all the calls and the messages, then put in a call to Toni, knowing she would be in the office by now. She walked out into the sunshine, listening to a dialling note and ringtone that sounded foreign, although the voice that answered was reassuringly familiar.

"Agatha, are you okay?" Toni asked. "We've been trying to get hold of you."

"I'm absolutely fine," Agatha answered, strolling out along the stone jetty in front of the hotel. "Don't worry about me."

"Where are you? You're not with John aboard the—"

"I don't want to talk about that, Toni. I'm fine, I'm safe, so let's get down to business . . ."

Reviewing their list of "things to do" didn't take long given that they'd spoken about it only the previous morning, although Toni had made good progress on the Sculley Security staff background checks.

"Patrick also found out that Sculley is divorced," she added. "The split from his wife is what prompted his move to Mircester."

"A fresh start, eh? Keep on him, Toni. See what you can dig up about him and that secretary of his. In the meantime, ask Patrick or Simon to find out all about Martin Randall. Keep it subtle. He's agreed to do the auction and Roy will deal with him on that, but I don't want him getting all huffy and pulling out. I got the feeling that he was taking more than just a polite interest in the burglaries and Mr. Tinkler's murder."

"You don't think he's a suspect, do you?"

"Everyone's a suspect until I've ruled them out in my own head," Agatha said ruefully. "You're one of very few people in the whole world that I trust right now, Toni. Maybe that's the way it should always have been."

Over the course of the next few days, Agatha kept in regular contact with Toni, who never again asked where she was or how she was feeling. She knew that was the way Agatha wanted it, and Agatha knew Toni had also briefed the rest of the staff to avoid those questions. Even when she spoke to Roy, who she could tell was itching to find out everything, he managed to stick to business.

Slowly, she settled into a routine that involved phone calls after breakfast, emails sent and received either at her desk or in the shade on her terrace until lunchtime, then a stroll into Puerto Pollensa along its famous Pine Walk promenade. The Pine Walk was lined with some fine villas built a century before as seaside retreats by wealthy holidaymakers from Palma and the mainland, and she enjoyed studying them as she walked by. Yet she had to keep her wits about her. The ancient, storm-battered pine trees that gave the Pine Walk its name leaned at odd angles along a string of small beaches and pushed up the maze of promenade paving stones with their roots, making it tricky in high heels. Agatha's daily routine crossing the cobbled lane to her office now paid dividends.

Closer to the centre of town, the Pine Walk widened, the villas and apartments giving way to restaurants and shops. The most colourful of the shops sold the kind of inflatable flamingos, beach towels, toys and newspapers from across Europe that were endemic in any beach resort, although mixed in among them Agatha found a number of pleasingly upmarket jewellers and chic boutiques. Beyond the Pine Walk lay the marina and a more modern, broad promenade running between a quiet road and a wide beach of golden sand. Villas, apartments and a tempting selection of bars and restaurants stretched out on the opposite side of the road, although the kind of tower-block hotels that dominated resorts in other parts of the island were satisfyingly absent.

Agatha quickly learned that if taking a walk for the exercise, it was not advisable to enjoy a glass of sangria with her lunch because reviewing case files after her walk back to the hotel could easily result in an unintentional siesta. She scolded herself on the only occasion that happened. She was here to work, after all, not laze around. She took dinner in the hotel's excellent restaurant or out on the terrace if the evening was warm enough, or ambled along the Pine Walk to find somewhere different. The hotel staff and other guests were happy to recommend good restaurants, some of the guests, knowing she was on her own, even inviting her to join them. On the odd occasion she did so, she manoeuvred any conversation about work round to the public-relations world, maintaining, with some degree of truth, that she was a retired PR executive.

Spending her afternoons scouring the old case files, however, was proving fruitless, and she was bracing herself for another session on returning to the hotel after lunch one day when she spotted a red-and-yellow seaplane landing in the bay. She walked out along the stone jetty to watch the aircraft taxi across the water towards the military base on the headland over to her left. The plane, she had learned, was an icon of the town, a water bomber that scooped up a bellyful of seawater to drop on the hill fires that erupted during the hotter weather. She tutted and turned away. She knew she was using the novelty of watching the seaplane as a distraction to keep her from the files.

In general, there were far fewer visitors in the resort than at the height of summer, but the hotel's terrace bar was still a popular place to sit in the sun, or the shade, enjoying the view and a drink or two. Ladies in sundresses and gentlemen in shorts mixed with others in swimsuits and beach towels, their conversations and laughter drifting towards her as Agatha walked in from the jetty. She noticed one young, dark-haired woman wearing a simple, yet elegant, white cotton cover-up over a plain black swimsuit. From behind her large dark sunglasses she appeared to be watching Agatha approach. Then she stood and, from the way she moved, even before she had whisked off her sunglasses, Agatha knew exactly who it was.

"Claudette!" Agatha gasped. "What are you doing here?"

"Looking for Agatha Raisin," the young woman said, with a serious pout. "She is disappeared, you know."

Then she burst out laughing, rushed towards Agatha and threw her arms around her.

"It is so good to see you!" she squealed, suddenly a whirlwind of excitement. "Only *I* know to be finding you here! Come, sit, and we shall have the gin-tonics."

"How did you find me?" Agatha asked, taking a seat in the shade beside Claudette, then shuffling it slightly and hitching up her long summer dress a little to stretch her legs in the sun, just as Claudette was doing.

"Simple," Claudette replied, ordering their drinks from the waitress who had appeared at their table. "John could not find you at the airport or when he phoned every hotel he can find in Palma and nearby."

"He tried looking for me."

"Of course. He is very upset."

"So he should be."

"Maybe," Claudette said, giving a French shrug. "Is not my business. I am worried only for you. Toni phoned everyone to find you. Charles phoned me. I think if you are not in England, then you are still in Mallorca. So where would you go? I look at this." She produced a paperback copy of *Problem at Pollensa Bay* from the bag on the ground next to her chair. "You once tell me Agatha Christie is your favourite and she has written about Pollensa. She also stayed here at Illa d'Or, although in this story, she calls it Pino d'Or. So I think I find you here."

"You should be one of my detectives."

"I think I have more money making wine!" Claudette laughed.

Claudette promised to report back only that she had found Agatha and that all was well without telling anyone where she was. In return, Agatha explained all about the murder, the kidnap attempts and the riddles, agreeing to let Claudette help sift through old cases or, as she put it, "Exercise your little grey matter like a real detective." Agatha maintained her work routine with calls and emails in the morning, Claudette using that time to visit friends all over the island, with taxi-driver Miguel providing transport. In the afternoons, the two women talked through whatever Agatha had found in her old cases, either sitting on her terrace or at a table down by the water.

One morning at breakfast, Claudette sat sipping coffee and pointed to Agatha's phone.

"You have no business calls today," she said.

"What do you mean?" Agatha asked.

"It is Sunday again, Agatha," Claudette said, grinning. "You lose track of time, no? Nobody is in their offices."

"It's easy to forget what day it is here. I was going to ask Toni if there were any more files she could send," Agatha said, staring at her phone, "but there's really no point. I'll text her and tell her to take it easy today. If I don't, then she probably will go into the office trying to dredge up more cases, and we're getting nowhere with that."

"What about Big Jim? I read about him—a boxer. A dangerous man. He sent men to burn down your house, did he not?"

"He did, and they failed. Jim Sullivan knows better than to target me again. He knows if anyone even suspects he's involved in anything that might happen to

171

me, my people have enough on him to put him behind bars for life. He won't try anything like that again."

"Then there is Barbaneagra—Blackbeard—the Romanian gangster. He sounds a very terrible man."

"He is," Agatha agreed. "Valeriu Fieraru is his real name and he's a dangerous character, without a doubt, but if he wanted me dead, he'd take great pleasure in killing me himself. He would definitely want me to know that he was having his revenge—and revenge is one of the most powerful motives for murder. He wouldn't send two incompetent thugs after me. He'd want everyone to know he killed me, and use that as a warning about what happens if you cross him.

"Blackbeard may come for me one day, but none of what's happened is his style at all. That's really the problem with the majority of these old cases. The villains most likely to want to try to kill me would simply go ahead and get it done. Messing around with riddles certainly wouldn't enter their heads."

"And we should clear our heads!" Claudette announced brightly. "We should swim in the pool, dry off, dress nicely and take a taxi to Pollensa to visit the market."

"Why do we need a taxi? We're in Pollensa."

"We are in Puerto Pollensa. Pollensa town is a short drive inland from here."

"Confusing having two places with the same name."

"But it is so common on islands in the Mediterranean," Claudette explained. "Many years ago, there were pirates who would raid the port, steal anything of value and kidnap people to sell as slaves."

"William Harrison must have passed by the island on his way into slavery," Agatha commented. "If he ever actually was a slave."

"Aha, this is your Campden man," Claudette said, "and the mystery Charles has set for you."

"He hasn't exactly set it for me. It's an old story that—"

"I have heard him talking, Agatha." Claudette lowered her voice in conspiratorial manner. "He uses this story to hook you!" She swung a hooked finger across the table. "He thinks he can fish you like a trout! Sometimes he is a selfish person, you know?"

"I know," Agatha said, thinking quietly to herself. First Margaret and now Claudette were warning her about Charles's intentions towards her. Well, she'd had enough of being played for a fool by men and, however clever he thought he was, Sir Charles Fraith was no match for Agatha Raisin. "I can handle Charles. Now—tell me about the two towns."

"So the people built towns inland where they could flee when they saw pirate ships approaching." Claudette continued her story. "They could defend the towns out of range from the ships' guns and stay safe."

"I suppose pirates didn't take taxis," Agatha said, laughing, "but we have Miguel, so let's go raid the market!"

Miguel dropped them in the main street leading into Pollensa and within a couple of minutes they had walked into the older area of the town. As they drew closer to the market, more and more people, locals as well as tourists, crowded the roads and pavements and, just before they entered a narrow street where covered market stalls nestled in the shade, Agatha turned and looked up. Framed between the ancient stone walls of the buildings, a forested hill a thousand feet high towered on the outskirts of town with what looked like a castle at its summit.

"That is Puig de Maria," Claudette said. "The building at the top is a chapel and convent that is more than six hundred years old, although there haven't been any nuns there for four hundred years. There is a path you can walk. There is a café. You can even spend the night."

"Some other time, maybe," Agatha said, looking at the rock faces too precipitous even for the most determined Mallorcan pines. "How come you know so much about the island?"

"I visit a few times. I have many friends here from the show-jumping circuit. There are stables all over the island with beautiful horses, not the poor, tired things forced to drag carriages in the resorts. It breaks my heart to see how sad some of those look. I hope the government will ban all the tourist carriages soon. Now, come and see the beautiful olives."

The food stalls in the market rampaged with colour, boasting locally grown peaches, peppers, olives, lemons, melons—just about every kind of fruit or vegetable you could think of as well as hams, cheeses, pies and pastries of all shapes and sizes. Other stalls sold clothes, linen, ceramics, jewellery and all manner of souvenirs.

Eventually, Agatha and Claudette battled their way through the crowds of marketgoers to the main square outside the cathedral. Agatha was about to claim a table at a restaurant when Claudette took her hand, coaxing her into a side street past the last of the stalls. They stopped at the bottom of a long flight of stone steps, as wide as the street, that disappeared up a steep slope. The age-old stones were polished smooth with the tread of countless footsteps.

"The Calvari Steps!" Claudette introduced Agatha to the dramatic stairway. "There is one step for each day of the year and a chapel at the top. We can do them for exercise . . . or take a seat in the shade for a nice, cool gin-tonic!"

"Shade for me," Agatha said, fanning herself with her sun hat. "Today is the hottest it's been."

They sat at one of the cafés at the foot of the Calvari Steps, sipping their drinks, when the sound of ringing bells filled the air. Agatha stared up at the cathedral bell tower, where the hands on the ornate black-and-white clockface indicated one o'clock.

"You are worried about the time?" Claudette asked.

"Not worried, just a little guilty. I feel like I'm on holiday and I really shouldn't be wasting time . . . wait a minute . . . wasting time . . . what did that last riddle say?"

She grabbed her phone and found a photograph she had taken of the third riddle.

"Look at this, Claudette," she said, then read it out loud. "'Give and take: You may give it but should never waste it. If I take it I will never have it. You may remember it but not all of it. Yours can only go onwards but I will end it.'"

"Yes, we know these words," Claudette said, frowning at the image.

"But we've been assuming it's about life—giving your life, taking a life and so on—but I don't think it is! What if it's about time? You can give your time to something but you should never waste your time. If you take your time, you'll never have enough time. You can remember times in the past, but not all of them."

"Yes, maybe," Claudette said, nodding, "but then it says your time 'can only go onwards, but I will end it.' Is still a death threat, no?"

"Perhaps," Agatha said, "but *time* is the real clue here, and that points to just one thing—the clock. These death-threat riddles started appearing after I bought the clock. When Mr. Tinkler was murdered, the only thing missing from the shop was the clock. They came for the clock having seen it in his shop window, but it wasn't there, so they tried to get him to tell them where it was.

"His brother had picked it up earlier that day, but Mr. Tinkler was never going to put Tristan in danger by telling them he had the clock. He died protecting his twin brother!"

"Then those same two men try to kidnap you. They want you to give them the clock!"

"But they didn't send these notes. The notes are a different game."

"Who would want your clock so badly, Agatha?"

"Who indeed?" Agatha keyed a contact number on her phone. "Hello, Martin, it's Agatha. I'm so sorry to be bothering you on a Sunday, but something rather urgent has come up."

Far from being perturbed by having his day of rest disturbed, Martin Randall sounded delighted to hear from her, asking only what he could do to help.

"I need to know who the other three bidders were when I bought the clock. I need their addresses," Agatha said.

"I'm sorry, but I can't actually tell you that, I'm afraid," Randall apologised.

"I realise that it might be confidential information . . ." Agatha said, preparing to use her auction agreement with Randall as a bargaining tool.

"I suppose it could be," Randall said, "but the form they sign makes it clear we can share their details with our partners for marketing purposes, and you're now a partner so I *can* share it with you, but it's on the office system, so I can't get at it until tomorrow morning. I'll email it to you."

"Tomorrow morning will be fine," Agatha said, grinning. She rang off and immediately made another call. "Toni, it's me. I'm coming home."

Agatha arrived back in Lilac Lane to find Roy and James waiting on her doorstep. Toni had picked her up from the airport and within minutes all four were sitting round the coffee table in her living room with glasses of rosé wine from a bottle Agatha had kept in a chiller sleeve all the way from Mallorca.

"It's from Can Vidalet," Agatha said. "A vineyard just outside Pollensa. Even Claudette liked it, and she knows her stuff."

They clinked glasses.

"Welcome home," Roy said, sipping the wine. "So what's the plan?"

Agatha looked at him in astonishment.

"You thought I'd want all the tittle-tattle?" he said, pursing his lips. "Well, I know I'll wheedle all that out of you eventually, but you didn't suddenly decide to rush home and spend all that time waiting at the airport and sitting on the plane without coming up with a plan. I know my Raisin, darling."

James laughed and reached out to touch Agatha's hand.

"He's got your number, my dear!" he said. "So what *is* the plan?"

"Roy," she said, smiling, happy to be back in the thick of things. "I'm glad you asked first. You did a bit of amateur dramatics, didn't you?"

"Always the understudy, never the lead," he replied, holding the back of his hand to his forehead for dramatic effect, "and, therefore, the one who was stuck with stage management and special effects."

"Good," Agatha said. "Toni, remember the theatrical costume place in Steventon where we hired our outfits for that ridiculous masked ball at Barfield House? I'll need you to pay them a visit tomorrow. James, you're pretty handy with a screwdriver and spirit level, aren't you?"

"No one in Carsely has straighter bookshelves than I do," James boasted.

"How are you on curtain rails?" Agatha asked.

"And no one has curtains that run more smoothly," James said, chuckling.

"Excellent," Agatha said, sitting back and taking a sip of rosé. "The Great Barfield Extravaganza is now less than a fortnight away. Before the fun begins there, we have a couple of traps to set."

Agatha was ready to leave for work the following morning, standing in the hall having yelled up the stairs twice to hurry Roy, when her phone rang. It was Tristan Tinkler.

"Agatha, I'm in the shop," he said. "Don't worry, no one saw me arrive. I came in last night and slept on an old camp bed."

"What are you doing at the shop?" Agatha asked, with a hint of annoyance. She had plans for the shop that morning and didn't want a secret lodger getting in the way.

"Toni told me you were back, and I have something to show you—I've got the clock working."

"I'll be there in half an hour. Don't come to the door. I'll let myself in with the spare keys you gave me," Agatha told him and said goodbye before bellowing to Roy. "Silver! Get your arse in gear or I'm leaving without you!"

While Agatha had been away, Toni and Helen Freedman had dealt with her car, which had been leased through Raisin Investigations. The wreck had been taken away and a brand-new car, an almost identically nondescript grey saloon, had been left in its place. As a private detective, when tailing a suspect or on observation, she needed a car that would be unnoticeable, one that wouldn't attract any attention. With Roy safely in the passenger seat, she set off down Lilac Lane.

When they reached the antiques shop, Agatha opened the door and called hello. The door and window blinds were down so no one could see in, and there was just one dim light struggling to banish the gloom at the back of the shop. Roy gasped when Tristan walked into the light. He hadn't known Timothy Tinkler well, but the sight of a dead man walking still took his breath away. Agatha, too, even though she now knew Tristan, was struck by the eerie sight of him there in the shop and shivered slightly when a chill swept through her.

"Come and see this," Tristan said, waving them forward to the back of the shop. "You'll be amazed!"

Agatha introduced Roy and they sat in front of the desk on which stood the golden clock, gleaming in the soft light and emitting a reassuring tick. Tristan then switched on another light so they could best admire his work.

"Obviously I've cleaned up the outside," Tristan said, hovering over the clock, "but there was some real work needed on the mechanism. When years of dust mixes with oiled parts, it starts to act as an abrasive, and some of the housings for the gears were over a millimetre . . ."

Agatha looked at him with an expression of barely concealed disinterest. Tristan chortled.

"All right, all you really need to know is that the clock mechanism is working perfectly," he went on, "but this clock has another two mechanisms, hence the three winding arbors. At first, I couldn't get at either of the others for fear of breaking something, but some friends of mine X-rayed it for me."

"I didn't think you could X-ray metal," Agatha said.

"It's an industrial process," Tristan explained. "They use it in engineering to find cracks inside machine parts and suchlike. The second mechanism runs the chimes and . . . well, just watch."

He opened the framed glass over the clockface and set the hands to three o'clock, whereupon the chimes began to pick out a simple tune. He gently closed the glass so his audience could enjoy the full spectacle.

"That's 'Wiener Carneval,'" Agatha said. "An early Strauss waltz—"

"Wait," Tristan said, holding up a hand to shush her. "Just watch."

Agatha caught her breath as the two dancers began to turn on their pedestal in time with the music and rise up, the pedestal becoming a spinning platform. They paused momentarily when their platform had reached the giddy height of about half an inch and three distinct chimes rang out. The dancers then descended back into place, twirling to the music and coming to rest as they were before when the waltz chimes stopped.

"That is utterly delightful," Roy said, clearly genuinely impressed.

Agatha said nothing. In her mind, the dancers had always been her and John. She was fighting back a tear and, for the moment, dared not speak. Fortunately, Tristan's enthusiasm for the clock swept her embarrassment aside unnoticed.

"There's more," he said, opening the glass once more.

"You can pull the minute hand out a bit." He gripped the minute hand at its base and gently eased it out a little. "I think that it now engages the third mechanism. Listen."

Tristan twisted his wrist so that the minute hand turned, giving a loud click as it passed each number on the clockface.

"You only hear the clicks when you go clockwise," Tristan demonstrated by returning the minute hand to twelve, "not when you turn it back. It feels almost like—"

"The combination lock on a safe," Agatha interrupted, back in control, without the slightest waver in her voice.

"Exactly!" Tristan was fired with excitement. "Wonderful, isn't it?"

"But what does it do?" Roy asked.

"Clearly it has something to do with the third mechanism," Tristan said, "but even on the X-rays we couldn't figure out what that was for."

"All we need is the combination," Agatha pointed out. "The correct sequence of numbers."

"But there are twelve numbers on the dial," Roy said. "How do we find the combination? There could be any number of sequences of up to twelve numbers. That would be . . ."

"More than four hundred and seventy-nine million options—and that's without repeating numbers," Tristan said. "My engineer pals are maths geeks."

"We could spend a lifetime trying to guess the right numbers," Roy said.

"Several lifetimes," Tristan added.

"Maybe we don't need to guess. Music and numbers

go hand in hand," Agatha said, focusing on the clock and thinking hard. "Some musicians can barely form words into a sentence on paper, yet they're often good with numbers and can read music from the page as if they're fluent in a language that is almost a language of numbers. They can hear those notes playing in their heads and count it out quite naturally, so they know exactly how fast or how slowly it should play."

"Agreed," Tristan said. "But how does that help us?"

"We have a number puzzle—the combination," Agatha said, talking more quickly as she felt a solution begin to materialise in her head. "We have some music—a waltz. I think the waltz could be a clue. Yes! Look at the whole clock. Now look at the illustrations on the three enamel panels. On the left are three dancers. In the centre panel are three posies of three delicate little flowers. On the right there are another three dancers. I think this is all down to the numbers of the waltz—the famous one-two-three, one-two-three, one-two-three rhythm. Tristan, I assume the dancers will stay up longest when the clock is striking twelve?"

"They will," Tristan agreed.

"Can you set the clock to twelve, please, then pull out the minute hand again so we can try a combination?"

Tristan did as he was asked, the "Wiener Carneval" played, and the dancers rose to the height of their platform. He then carefully pulled the minute hand forward and offered Agatha the chance to enter a combination. She moved the hand until it clicked on the number one, then two, then three, then repeated the process a second and third time. She sat back, and what happened next made her eyes open wide in wonder.

Simon was the first to greet Agatha and Roy when they walked into the office, jumping up from his seat as soon as they walked into the room.

"Welcome home, boss!" he cheered, his thin face wrinkling into a wide grin. "Good to have you back . . . um . . . Are you two okay?"

"Yes, yes, fine, thank you, Simon," Agatha said, looking as though she were lost in thought.

"Coffee . . ." Roy said, then veered off towards the kitchen in something of a daze. Agatha's phone then rang, saving her from any further questions.

"Good morning, Agatha!" came Martin Randall's buoyant greeting. "I've sent you those names and addresses. I don't actually know any of the bidders. The first two are fairly local, but the third is a complete red herring."

"What do you mean?" Agatha asked, blinking hard and giving her head a shake to focus on the call.

"The third bidder gave her details only as H. E. M. Kiesler, Vienna. Clearly a fake."

"It sounds a bit dodgy, I'll give you that, but how do you know for certain it's not real?"

"Come on, Agatha!" Randall laughed. "I thought you were well versed in the most important women of the modern age. Hedwig Eva Maria Kiesler was a brilliant scientist from Vienna and one of the most beautiful women ever to walk the planet. Her inventions helped give us that mobile phone you're holding and when she hit Hollywood she became the most glamorous film star of all time—Hedy Lamarr."

"I see." Agatha nodded. "Well, she may not be Hedy Lamarr, but our third bidder is a woman I would very much like to meet. In the meantime, I'll have a word with the other two."

She ended the call and accepted a cup of coffee from Roy. Helen Freedman looked slightly affronted, as though part of her job description had just been usurped. She welcomed Agatha back, then, seeing her boss studying the addresses on her phone that Randall had just sent, she took the armful of papers she was carrying and added them to the stack already on Agatha's desk.

"Roy," Agatha said, looking round to where he was settling in to his desk. "James will be here shortly to help downstairs. Simon, Patrick, I'd like you two to lend a hand as well. Tristan is downstairs. Simon will explain about him, Patrick. Roy will explain about the job. Everything else goes on hold—this is now our most important job."

"Can we show you one thing first, boss?" Simon sounded excited, so Agatha nodded. He beckoned her over to Patrick's computer, where Patrick called up images from the car park in the London hotel where Stuart Sculley had stayed.

"Simon and I have gone through hours of this stuff," Patrick said.

"Helps kill time on the nightshift." Simon laughed. Agatha looked at her watch and he could see her forbearance evaporating. "We found something strange."

"Just after midnight on the night Aurelia Barclay's shop was hit, this appeared," Patrick said, pointing to a motorbike driving round the exit barrier and speeding out of the car park.

"A motorbike," Agatha said. "Sneaking out round the barrier. So what?"

"So a motorbike left, but there's no footage of it arriving," Simon said, "and the hotel has no records of any guests parking a motorbike."

"We checked the licence plate," Patrick went on, "and the number is for a 2012 Kawasaki. The bike caught on camera is a 2019 Triumph Bonneville. The plates are fake."

"It's the same on each night there was a burglary," Simon said. "The motorbike leaves but never arrives."

"How could it leave without arriving?" Agatha said, frowning at the screen. "Much easier to leave a car park like that, of course. To get in, you'd have to check in to the hotel or have a pass. We need to give that some thought. Now, I have a couple of potential riddlers to visit."

"Not on your own," Toni said, standing at her side. "We're not letting you go anywhere on your own. I've been in touch with the costume place and I'm going there this afternoon. This morning, I'm with you."

"You can't . . ." Agatha was about to rail against being told what she could and couldn't do, but then relented.

It would be good to have Toni watching her back. "All right, Toni, let's go."

Stephen Samuels's home was the first address they visited. A two-storey Victorian villa built in the ubiquitous, mellow Cotswold stone, the house stood in a neat garden on the edge of Ancombe. When they rang the doorbell it was answered by a man who looked to be in his seventies, with thinning red hair—most definitely the man who had been bidding from the middle of the auction floor.

"It's Mrs. Raisin, isn't it?" said Stephen Samuels, the words tumbling out of his mouth through a barrier of prominently crooked teeth. "I've seen your picture in the paper and I saw you at that auction. You live over in Carsely, don't you? Please, do come in, both of you."

Agatha introduced Toni, Samuels then leading them into a wide hallway where a door to the left stood open and a cacophony of ticking billowed out. Samuels reached for the door handle, then saw Agatha eyeing the room.

"It's where I tinker," he said, the teeth putting in another appearance. "I find the ticking of the clocks quite relaxing, like music, but I know not everyone agrees! Take a look, if you like."

Agatha stood in the doorway, leaning in to scan the room. At one time, it might have been a dining room but now it was devoted entirely to Samuels's passion. There were clocks everywhere—clocks of all shapes and sizes. Grandfather clocks stood tall on the floor, while others littered shelves, tables and every other available space, including a workbench where one mantel clock lay in pieces under a powerful desk light, like a patient on an operating table.

Samuels motioned her to step aside, then closed the door, cutting the ticking noise to a more comfortable level.

"I don't like people going in there," he said. "I've got all my bits and pieces laid out on my bench and, well, accidents happen. I can't stand the thought of losing some of those little cogs and screws. That could spell disaster."

"I'm sure it could," Agatha agreed. "It's a real racket in there, though. What happens when they all start chiming?"

"That would be very, very loud," Samuels said, his eyes wide and his head nodding. "So I disable a lot of the chimes. Even I couldn't stand that!"

He showed them into a spacious drawing room with intricate cornicing on the ceiling and a large, marble fireplace on which stood an elaborate vase and two matching carriage clocks. Despite the warmer weather outside, a couple of logs were burning gently in the grate. The room was a peaceful sanctuary compared to the workroom opposite, with just the regular, soft, "tick-tock" of the tallest grandfather clock Agatha had ever seen spreading an aura of calm. The brass pendulum swung hypnotically in its glass-fronted case, and the clock's large face, gleaming with silvered brass, was engraved with swirling patterns that drew your eyes around their intricate paths.

"That's just beautiful," Toni said, standing in front of the clock.

"Yes, it is, isn't it?" Samuels said and smiled, the teeth bursting out of his mouth once again. "There are other clocks in this room," he added, waving an arm as though introducing them all, "but they run almost silently because all I ever want to hear in here is this one. My missus was the same. Betty loved that clock—that's why I keep her in here."

He pointed to the vase, Agatha and Toni suddenly realising that it wasn't simply a vase, but an urn containing his deceased wife's ashes. Samuels invited them to sit on a comfortable sofa in front of the fire before hurrying off to make tea, which he served in china mugs.

"I suppose you want to ask me about the clock at the auction," he said, lowering himself into an armchair.

"We do," Agatha said. "You dropped out of the bidding—why?"

"Because it was all getting out of hand, Mrs. Raisin. You and that other woman were offering far too much money. If it was in perfect condition, that clock might have been worth what you paid, but it was far from perfect."

"I've been assured that it can be repaired—" Agatha began before Samuels interrupted her.

"Oh, it's not just that. There's something weird about it."

"Weird? What do you mean?" Toni asked.

"Well, the dancing couple on the top—something odd about them." He paused and sipped his tea with a slurping sound, as though straining it through his teeth. "Then there's those panels—the enamelled bits. I can't quite figure out what they're all about."

"Surely they're just there for decoration—because

189

they're pretty," Agatha said, suddenly feeling the need to defend her precious clock.

"They're pretty enough, I suppose," Samuels said, "but they make the whole thing a bit bulky, when the whole form of the thing would have worked better slimmed down."

Agatha now felt that her beloved clock was under attack for being . . . plump. She wasn't about to take that from someone who looked like he was chewing on a mouthful of piano keys.

"What I want to know is . . ." she began, but Toni had seen the outburst building and subtly laid a restraining hand on Agatha's arm.

"What has really been perplexing us, Mr. Samuels," she said, "is how we can talk to the other bidders. You're quite well-known as a clock expert, but we want to find out more about the history of the clock and we thought they might be able to shed some light on it."

"Made in Paris, they said, but that's part of its problem," Samuels said. "Not enough history. To me, it looked a bit more German than French . . ."

"Austrian, maybe?" Agatha suggested.

"Could well be, Mrs. Raisin," Samuels said, nodding. "Can't say much more about it than that without taking it to bits, though."

"Did you know any of the other bidders?" Toni asked.

"Never seen the woman before," Samuels said, "but the bloke up at the back was Henry Milner. He's got a place on the Mircester road. Fancies himself as a horologist but he doesn't know a mainspring from a kick in the arse, if you'll pardon my French."

"Is this him?" Toni said, showing Samuels the image from Agatha's security camera.

"That's him all right. I'd recognise those specs anywhere."

Agatha looked at Toni, a thin smile playing on her lips. The riddler was now in their sights.

Chapter Nine

Henry Milner's house was a small, dull, brick-built bungalow in a cluster of modern houses that all looked exactly alike, huddled in a cul-de-sac off the Mircester Road. Agatha parked in the street by Milner's front gate, then walked up the short garden path with Toni. Milner's front door swung open when they were still a couple of paces away, and he stood on the threshold, a smarmy smile on his face.

"Ah, Mrs. Raisin!" he said, with a welcome about as warm as a wet penguin. "Do come in. I've been expecting you."

"He's unbelievable," Agatha said quietly to Toni, following Milner into his sitting room. "He thinks he's some kind of super villain!"

The room was comfortably furnished with a beige sofa and an armchair, either side of a small fireplace equipped with a flame-effect electric fire. On the mantelpiece and on a sideboard that stood against one wall were several clocks of various sizes. Milner sat in a black office chair at a writing desk by the window, swinging the chair round to face Agatha and Toni, who seated themselves on the sofa. Without taking his eyes off them, he gently pushed his desk drawer closed, positioning himself protectively in front of it.

"I must say, I didn't think it would take you quite so long to find me," Milner said, smirking. "Agatha Raisin, the great detective . . ."

"I wasn't really trying," Agatha said. "I didn't think you were worth the bother and, as it happens, you're not."

"Yet here you are," he said, an unpleasant look crossing his face, "beating a path to my door."

"This isn't a courtesy call," Agatha pointed out. "I'm here to put an end to your silly little game. It was all about the clock, wasn't it?"

"A woman like you doesn't deserve to own a clock like that!" Milner rasped, his temper roused. "How could someone like you ever appreciate such a wonderful work of art? You think you can just splash your money around and get whatever you want! That clock should be owned by someone who can look after it properly, not a trollop like you!"

Agatha made to rise from the sofa, but Toni placed a restraining hand on her arm.

"You couldn't have the clock, so you didn't want Agatha to enjoy having it, either," Toni said. "You wanted to make her unhappy. That's why you sent the riddles."

"Riddles?" Milner shrugged his shoulders. "What riddles? You can't prove a thing."

"We've got you on camera, you moron!" Agatha snarled, leaping to her feet and lunging forward, grabbing hold of his chair. "And nobody gets away with threatening me, even if a little weasel like you could never make good on the threat!"

She spun the chair and pushed it aside, Milner clinging to the arms.

"What's in here that you were so keen to make sure we didn't see?" she asked, yanking open the desk drawer. A scattering of small, square envelopes lay in the drawer along with a selection of half-finished riddles. Agatha stared down at the cowering Milner.

"You're pathetic," she said.

"You can't go through my personal things like that!" Milner wailed. "You can't touch anything in here!"

"Maybe not," Agatha said, looking out the window towards the street, "but they can."

Bill Wong and a uniformed constable had just stepped out of a police car.

"Sending threats or malicious messages is a crime, Mr. Milner," Agatha said, watching Toni open the front door to Bill. "You're going to jail."

"Will he really go to prison?" Toni asked once they were back on the road to the office. "I'm not sure he's tough enough to survive on the inside."

"He'll probably get off with a fine and a suspended sentence," Agatha assured her. "I don't want to spend another second thinking about him. I said the riddles were a waste of time and I was right. Now we have far more important things to think about."

After parking the car, Agatha paused outside the antiques shop before taking the stairs to her office. The interior of the shop was now obscured by a black curtain that stretched from floor to ceiling. The shop window had been cleared of antiques and dressed entirely in black velvet. On a plinth set back from the window to the left was a framed photograph of Mr. Tinkler with a simple sign below it bearing the dates of his birth and death. On an identical plinth to the right was Agatha's clock with another sign announcing it was to be auctioned at the Great Barfield Extravaganza. Agatha sighed. It seemed in very poor taste to be advertising the extravaganza alongside the tribute to Mr. Tinkler, but the end would justify the means.

Upstairs in Raisin Investigations, Roy was waiting to report to Agatha.

"The boys are still working behind the scenes downstairs," he said. "We're expecting some more curtain material to be delivered later. We'll bring that in the back way. And these have just arrived."

Roy handed Agatha three copies of the auction catalogue for the Great Barfield Extravaganza.

"Excellent!" Agatha said, flicking through the pages illustrated with expensive watches and jewellery. "Martin's done a good job. I'll take one with me when I pay another visit to Stuart Sculley this afternoon."

"Can we make that as soon as I get back from the costume place?" Toni said. "We may have seen off the riddler, but you're not out of the woods yet."

Agatha gave a resigned nod and promised to go no-where without Toni. In her office, she took a look at the pile of paperwork on her desk, ignored it and reached for her phone. After the usual bout of jousting with Gustav, she was put through to Charles.

"Great to have you back, Aggie!" Charles said, and Agatha took a deep breath, determined not to have the conversation derailed by a spat about the pet name. They talked about the ongoing preparations for the extravaganza, and then Agatha plunged into the real reason for her call.

"I know you have more rooms in Barfield than you can count," she said, "so I was wondering if you would host a house guest until after the extravaganza."

"Of course," Charles said. "Who is it?"

"It's Timothy Tinkler's brother, Tristan," Agatha said. "I need him to be kept out of the way for a while, although he'll be doing a sort of nightshift with us. I can explain properly later."

"Sounds interesting," Charles said, "and I'll help any way I can. How are you doing? I take it things didn't go as you wanted on the cruise ship?"

"I don't want to get into that, Charles. We have far too many other things to concentrate on."

"Yes, yes, of course," Charles said, immediately aware that he had touched a raw nerve. "I'll have Gustav prepare a room for Tristan."

It was late afternoon when Agatha and Toni walked into Stuart Sculley's office, Yvonne showing them in and promising to return with tea and chocolate digestives.

"I thought you might be interested in these," Agatha said, once they had dispensed with their greetings. She handed an extravaganza auction catalogue and events programme across the desk to Sculley. "I've been staggered at the response we've had not only from those who are helping to make the whole day such a special event, but from people who have donated so generously to the charity auction."

"I can see," Sculley said, browsing the catalogue. "Some very nice pieces here."

"We don't actually have them all yet," Toni said, "but everything will be brought together at Barfield the afternoon before the big day."

"You should see the wonderful old safe Sir Charles has in his study!" Agatha laughed. "It's like something you'd see in a movie. The room's actually the library and there's a portrait that swings out from the wall and this huge safe is right there, embedded in the brickwork."

"Sounds like he could use some security advice," Sculley said, smiling.

"That's the whole point," Agatha replied. "All of the great and the good titled aristocrats from far and wide will be there at the extravaganza and they all have these creaky old mansions that always look to me like a burglar's delight. I know how badly you've been hit by the break-ins, so I thought you should come along to the extravaganza, make some new contacts and maybe pick up some business."

"That's a great idea," Sculley agreed. "Would you be able to make a few introductions for me?"

"Of course," Agatha said. "We can start with Sir

Charles himself. Barfield House could definitely use a security upgrade."

They talked over tea, Agatha refusing the tempting chocolate biscuits, and less than an hour later, she and Toni were on their way back to the office.

"Did you see his eyes light up when he saw the catalogue?" Toni said.

"I did," Agatha replied. "He's clearly a man who appreciates expensive things."

"There have been no burglaries since Aurelia Barclay's, and they didn't get away with anything there," Toni pointed out. "With nothing to sell on, the burglars may be starting to run low on cash."

"I'm counting on it," Agatha said.

"Is Martin Randall still a suspect?"

"I don't entirely trust Mr. Randall," Agatha said, mulling over the question in her head, "but neither do I trust Stuart Sculley or his London alibi. One way or another, we'll see a result on the burglaries before the extravaganza."

Two days passed, and the activity around the extravaganza went into overdrive. Agatha spent much of her time at Barfield House, personally supervising the construction of a catwalk and curtained backstage area for the fashion show. She was standing with an engineer, talking about the sound system, when Gustav appeared by her side, accompanied by Mrs. Tassy.

"It's all rather exciting, isn't it?" Mrs. Tassy warbled.

"There hasn't been so much activity around here since Charles married that hideous Darlinda woman."

"I have just spoken with someone who wants to land a biplane in the top field," Gustav said, sounding appalled.

"That's right," Agatha said. "Charles agreed. We have all the right permits. The pilot's giving an aerobatics display."

"How thrilling." Mrs. Tassy clapped her hands in delight. Agatha had never seen the old lady so animated. "The last time an aeroplane landed there was when Spotty Milton flew his Spitfire in back in 1944. I was just a girl, but I'll never forget it."

"They're going to park old cars on the lawn and drive steam engines back and forth. The grass will take weeks to recover. I take it there will be no children at the event?" Gustav said, spitting out the word "children" as though it were poison. "I don't want an army of screaming urchins running all over the place."

"I'm sure children would love some of the things at the extravaganza," Agatha said, "but it's basically all centred around launching a brand of booze, Gustav, so we're advising guests to leave their kids at home. Hopefully that means they can let their hair down a bit, too."

"Let their . . . ? Oh, that's just wonderful, isn't it? That's all we need—a rave!" He wandered off towards the sanctuary of his butler's pantry muttering to himself about drunks throwing up in his flowerbeds.

"Don't worry about him, Mrs. Raisin," said Mrs. Tassy. "He's just an old stick-in-the-mud. He's used to being in control here and doesn't like it when others take over."

"I'll talk to him," Agatha said. "I may need his help with a couple of . . . confidential and delicate matters that will make him feel more involved."

"Wonderful!" Mrs. Tassy turned for the library, almost skipping with excitement. "All this and dark intrigue as well!"

It was a late and dismal Mircester night when the last of the King Charles's customers took his final sip of ale and bumbled off up the lane towards the high street. The bar manager threw the bolts on the door and could then be seen through the dimpled glass windows along with one of her staff, wiping tables, cleaning glasses and running a vacuum cleaner across the floor. When even they had finally finished their long day's work and headed home, the old lane fell silent. What warmth had penetrated the gloomy lane when the sun briefly reached between the buildings during the day had vanished as the damp chill of night descended. Wisps of moisture could be seen drifting through the anaemic veils of street light and where the winding lane's twists and turns rendered the lights almost ineffective, it was as though nothing had changed in centuries.

A quiet cough, muffled by the dank air, announced a presence and a black-clad figure stepped out of the shadows. The first was followed by a second, both wearing balaclavas that covered their faces, and together they moved stealthily towards the antiques shop. They paused to look in through the window, studying the clock that stood on its velvet plinth, delicately uplit by an unseen spotlight. Nodding to each other, they swiftly approached the shop's entrance, crouching in the shelter of the doorway where one produced a heavy crowbar. There was a rasping sound of splintering, tearing wood, and the shop door cracked open, the crowbar clattering to the floor.

The two figures dashed inside towards the clock but had taken no more than two paces when the spotlight was extinguished, plunging them into complete darkness. They froze, hearing a sinister swish of movement, then shielded their eyes when they were suddenly illuminated by bright spotlights somewhere above them. All around was totally black bar the spot where they were standing, and the clock, along with its plinth, was gone.

"What is this?" hissed one of the figures. "What's goin' on?"

"Search me," replied the other. "I'm out of here . . . but where's the door gone?"

He made to move in roughly the direction he thought he had arrived, but a voice boomed out of the darkness.

"Stay!"

They froze, and black nooses were instantly dropped over their heads down to their chests and pulled tight, pinning their arms to their sides. One began to spin and kick but was knocked to the ground by an unseen foe who swept his legs from under him. The other looked on in horror before being felled himself. Their ankles were quickly bound and their hands fastened behind them with the telltale clicking noise of cable ties tightening. Then the voice came again.

"Kneel!"

They were dragged to their knees and the balaclavas were torn from their heads. One of the men was dark-haired, with a round face and sparse stubble that made him look barely beyond his teenage years. The other was slightly younger, with lighter hair and vivid acne rashes searing each side of his face. Both were now wide-eyed with terror.

"Behold the Angels of Darkness!" came the voice and two women stepped forward from the blackness to the edge of the light. Each was wearing a full-length black cloak that revealed a dark red lining when they moved. With their heads slightly bowed, the hoods of their cloaks hid their faces, but on prominent display were the shining swords each of them was using both hands to hold upright in front of them.

"Let me out of here!" howled the acned youth.

"Silence!" commanded one of the Angels, "lest the Angels smite off your heads!"

Both the men stared up at the swords, the younger one with his lower lip trembling.

"You have invaded the inner sanctum," the Angel accused them, "and you must pay for your crimes. Turn to face your accuser!"

A swishing noise from behind the two kneeling men prompted them to shuffle round to see that the blackness of the room had extended to an area where white smoke

202

now blossomed under another bright light. Then, into the illuminated smoke stepped Mr. Tinkler, wearing a beige cardigan and baggy brown trousers and staring at them over his half-moon glasses looking very, very annoyed. In his hands he held a wicked-looking battleaxe.

"No!" screamed the older of the two. "You're not real! You died!"

Mr. Tinkler slammed the battleaxe into the ground and they felt the reverberations through their knees. He left them in no doubt that he was real. The younger one was whimpering.

"We didn't mean it . . ." he whispered. "We didn't mean to kill you . . ."

"He who cannot be killed may not die," said the voice. "Your lives, however, now lie in the balance. Answer my questions truthfully and you may yet leave this place alive."

"What questions?" asked the older captive.

"Who sent you here?" the Angel asked.

"The woman," cried the younger one. "She sent us. She made us do it!"

"What is her name?"

"We don't know," said the younger one. "Honest! We don't know!"

There was a roar of fury and Mr. Tinkler stepped towards the men, the battleaxe raised. The Angels quickly stepped round their prisoners, putting themselves between Mr. Tinkler and his targets, crossing their swords in front of him, holding him back.

"Murderers!" he shrieked. "Murderers!"

"Tristan," Agatha spoke quietly and calmly from

beneath the hood of her Angel cloak, pushing it back slightly so she could look Tristan in the eye. She kept her voice low to prevent the kneeling thugs from hearing. "Keep your head. Follow the plan. Much as they deserve it, we can't let you at them. We need them to help us find the woman. Step back. It's time for you to disappear again."

He looked at her, looked back at the two youths, then nodded before backing away into the swirling smoke. Agatha turned and her fellow Angel followed suit. They took two paces forward to stand in front of the men. Agatha then flung back her hood and stood with her hands on the hilt of her sword, its point resting on the floor. She nodded to the other Angel who revealed herself as Toni.

"You two!" the younger man breathed. "Who the hell are you people?"

"You have no idea what you're dealing with here," she said, staring down at them with a grave expression. "Those we serve could snuff out your lives in an instant. Tell us what we need to know or our faces in the darkness of this sanctum will be the last thing you ever see!"

"Who are you?" Toni asked.

"I'm Jez," said the older one. "He's Reggie."

"I don't need to know who *they* are!" Agatha barked, making sure their prisoners felt her theatrical anger. "They're dead men! They mean nothing anymore unless they can tell us who the woman is!"

"We'll tell you everything," said Jez, "but we don't know who she is!"

"How long have you worked for her?" Toni asked.

"We don't really work for her," Reggie wailed. "It's not like she gave us real jobs or anythin' . . ."

Agatha snarled, "Stop wasting my time. Where did you meet her?"

"She came up to us when we were hangin' out, havin' a smoke down by the ruins," said Jez. Agatha knew the spot. The ruined part of the old abbey was a favourite with local Mircester kids smoking weed. "She said we could make some easy money. All we had to do was bust into the shop and take the clock off the old man."

"But he didn't have the clock, did he?" Agatha said, now channelling her real anger into the performance. "So you beat him to death!"

"I swear we didn't mean for him to die!" Reggie squeaked, then pointed to the smoke where he had last seen Tristan. "And, well . . . he didn't, did he?"

"You have no idea of the dark forces at work here," Toni said, warming to the occult theme. "Just answer truthfully. Did the woman tell you to come after us?"

"Not you. Just her," Jez said, nodding towards Agatha. "When the clock wasn't here, we were told to get you to tell us where it was."

"Did you always meet down by the ruins?" Agatha asked.

"No, we never seen her again," Jez said. "Haven't even spoke to her. She gave us a mobile and sends us texts."

"How does she pay you?" Toni asked.

"She sends a text tellin' us where she's left an envelope of cash," Reggie said.

"Where's the phone?" demanded Agatha.

"In my back pocket," Jez said.

Agatha looked past him into the darkness and gave a small nod. The next thing Jez and Reggie knew, they were blindfolded and had tape slapped over their mouths.

"You will be taken from this place," Agatha informed them, "to be interred until the time comes for you to face . . . um . . ." She looked to Toni for inspiration.

"Trial by fire!" Toni announced boldly. Agatha nodded her approval.

Headphones were put over the prisoners' ears and taped in place before Simon and Patrick stepped fully into the light. Simon plucked the mobile phone from Jez's back pocket and handed it to Agatha.

"What can they hear?" Agatha asked.

"Not a thing," Simon assured her, bending down to scream in Reggie's face as proof. There was no reaction.

"We can't keep them like that for long," Patrick said. "They're already terrified. It will drive them mad."

"It's just until we get them out of here," Agatha said. "I don't want them hearing anything we say."

"Trial by fire?" Simon said, looking at Toni and laughing. "What's that about?"

"I improvised to help out Agatha," Toni said, frowning at him. "By the look on their faces, it scared the crap out of them."

"So did 'smite off their heads,'" Patrick said. "Where did that come from?"

"I heard it on a TV cartoon show when I was channel flicking," Agatha said, smiling. "We have two frightened and confused young thugs here. We need to keep them that way until we get our hands on that bitch who sent them. We can't have them warning her off."

The normal shop lights came on and Roy appeared from behind one of the black drapes. He switched off the smoke machine, fanning a hand in front of his face.

"I'll open the back door to clear the air," he said, then looked down at the two bound and gagged prisoners with an expression of sheer disgust. "Scum. What do we do with them?"

"They deserve to suffer," Tristan said, walking through from the back of the shop. "They killed him! They killed Tim!"

"Right now, I'd say they're suffering, all right," Agatha said, standing by Tristan's side and putting an arm round his shoulders. They looked down at the two killers. The younger one was sobbing. "They'll go to prison eventually, and probably count themselves lucky at that. Until then, they'll be stuck in the world of our little charade."

She turned to the others.

"Right, let's get to work. We need to get these curtains down and have the shop back to normal by tomorrow morning. We need it to look like nothing happened here, and that includes repairing the front door. Simon, Patrick, stick those two on a couple of chairs to keep them out of the way."

She placed Jez's mobile on Mr. Tinkler's old desk and found her own in her handbag, keying in a speed-dial number.

"Charles," she said. "You can bring the van round now. We have two ready to go."

Charles was there within minutes, helping Agatha and Toni to bundle the two youths into the back of a white van used on his estate. Gustav was at the wheel.

"We can take off their headphones now," Agatha said, "but you and Gustav must keep quiet. I don't want them hearing your voices. They'll know Toni and me, but no one else."

"That's all very well," Charles said, "but they're going to tell everyone who'll listen about all of this. They'll tell the woman who's behind it all, and once she knows they're in custody, she'll head for the hills. She'll get clean away."

"We're taking these two to Mircester Police Station," Agatha said. "There, they will go inside and confess to the murder of Timothy Tinkler. Their stories will make about as much sense as John Perry's did all those years ago, but Bill Wong will take them seriously—I'll make sure of that.

"Their boss won't take off and leave the clock behind," Agatha continued. "I'm certain of that, and her two sidekicks can't warn her that they're in the cells because they only have one way of communicating with her—the phone she gave them—and I now have that."

Gustav stopped the van in an alleyway close to the police station but out of sight of any security cameras. The two thugs, their headphones removed and ankles freed, were led out into the street by Agatha and Toni, still in their black robes.

"You will walk the way you are now facing," Agatha ordered them. "You will walk to the police station and confess your crimes. You will remain silent until you get there and you will not look back. We will be watching you. Do you understand?"

Both men nodded.

"Do exactly as you have been told," Toni warned them. "There are many Angels who can reach you wherever you are. Fail to obey and you will face trial by fire!"

They removed the tape gagging the men, cut the ties at their wrists, then silently backed away into the alley, leaving the two killers to remove their own blindfolds. As soon as they did so, they ran straight to the police station and in through the doors. Gustav drove back towards Agatha's office, parking a safe distance away, and Charles walked with Agatha and Toni to the antiques shop's back entrance.

"I wonder how long it will take before I get a call from Bill?" Agatha smiled and, as if by magic, her phone rang.

"Agatha," came Bill's voice. "We have two characters down at the station who want to confess to the murder of Timothy Tinkler and are raving about you and something called the Angels of Darkness. Do you know anything about this?"

"Not a thing," Agatha said without hesitating over the lie for an instant, "but they sound dangerous. You should keep them locked up."

"We don't have much choice," Bill said. "Our desk officer thought they were just a couple of potheads and tried to sling them out, but they said the Angels would get them and insisted on being locked up. One of them then whacked the desk officer and the other started smashing up the reception area, so they're both now in the cells."

"Will they actually prosecute them for murder?" Charles asked when Agatha ended the call.

"With forensics and their confessions, even Wilkes

will be able to convict them," Agatha said. "They'll be locked up for a long time. Where was John Perry kept when he was first imprisoned?" she asked, suddenly curious.

"I think Perry was kept in the local lock-up for a while, and in the cellar of an inn. Neither was particularly secure. He couldn't get out, but people could easily chat to him or slip him the odd tankard of ale."

"Do we know who it was that told Perry about the indemnity law?"

"Given how many people may have had access to him, and his mother and brother, it's impossible to say."

A buzzing sound came from Agatha's handbag and she produced the phone she had taken from Jez. On it was a brief text message:

Have you got the clock?

Agatha thought for a second and then replied to the message.

Clock gone. Auction at Barfield House.

She smiled, dropping the phone back into her handbag. The charity auction was promising to be the highlight of the whole Great Barfield Extravaganza.

After another hectic day of preparations, Agatha was contemplating a gin and tonic to ease her way into the evening when her doorbell rang. She frowned. She wasn't expecting anyone. Strolling out into the hall, she peeked through the spyhole in her front door, wondering if she might see James, or perhaps Margaret. Who she *did* see brought a sharp intake of breath—Letitia.

"Snakes and bastards!" she hissed. "What the bloody hell is that tart doing here?"

Her immediate inclination was to fling open the door and smack the woman in the mouth. Then, she reasoned that the dancer must have very good cause to turn up on her doorstep. Her detective's instincts screamed at her to find out why. Her first thought then stirred itself into a whirlwind in her mind, blasting all reason aside. A smack in the mouth it was, then.

She yanked open the door, made to lunge at the younger woman, then stopped. Letitia had changed. This was not the over-polished glamour-puss she had encountered in Palma. This Letitia was almost devoid of make-up and was dressed in a plain, grey, lightweight rain jacket. Most remarkable of all, a tear was fighting its way down her cheek.

"Hello," she said weakly. "I guess I'm pretty much the last person you expected to see tonight."

"Not the last," Agatha said. "You didn't even make the list."

"You must hate me."

Agatha eyed her suspiciously. Her curiosity was now getting the better of her temper, but the anger was standing by as a backup.

"I'd like to say I don't care enough about you to hate you, but that would be wrong," she said, her jaw set firm. "I do hate you."

"I don't blame you. You've every right, but there's something you should know. Something I need to tell you."

"This 'something' must be very important to bring you all the way to my door."

"It is. I've done something really awful . . . I'm so ashamed of myself."

Letitia could hold back her tears no longer, breaking down and sobbing so hard that Agatha was sure she was going to collapse. These were not, to Agatha's expert eye, simple crocodile tears. This was not a performance, or, if it was, it was worthy of an Oscar. The woman was genuinely upset.

"You'd best come in," she said, stepping aside to let Letitia into the hall. "You're ruining the peace and quiet out there."

Letitia wiped her eyes with a tissue, smudging what little mascara she was wearing onto her cheeks. Agatha handed her a larger tissue from a box on her hall stand and Letitia blew her nose.

"Thank you," she said. "You're very kind. I imagined that, when you saw me here, you might just punch me on the nose."

"Don't worry. That can still be arranged."

"What I wanted to say is . . ." Letitia gave a little hiccup and a few more tears appeared.

"Oh, for goodness' sake!" Agatha snapped. "Whatever you want to say, I don't want to hear it without the gin and tonic I was about to make. Go sort yourself out in the little bathroom over there," she pointed to a door beneath the stairs, "and I'll make you one as well."

Letitia, Agatha judged, had made a reasonable job of composing herself and an equally reasonable job on her make-up repairs. She had left her rain jacket on the hall stand and was wearing a simple white T-shirt and jeans. She looked horribly fit, appallingly lithe and disgustingly slim. Agatha felt like flinging her gin and tonic over her, but restrained herself, handing her the drink gently instead. Despite the way she looked, there was something peculiarly vulnerable about this woman. Letitia sat on the sofa, Agatha in her armchair, and they each sipped their drinks.

"Come on then, spit it out," Agatha said, and immediately cursed herself for making it sound like Letitia should spit out the gin. "What is it you want to say?"

"I'll come straight to the point," Letitia replied, taking a deep breath. "Nothing happened between John and me. We danced demonstrations, he did his job and that was all. He was always very pleasant, but he had no interest in me as anything other than a colleague."

"You don't really expect me to believe that, do you? What's happened? Has he thought better of his little dalliance with you and sent you here to plead his case?"

"He doesn't know I'm here. He would be appalled if he thought we were talking. He won't have anything to do with me."

"That's not what it looked like on your 'love boat,'" Agatha said, leaning forward, her temper warming at the memory. "It looked very much like you were far more than just 'a colleague'!"

"Yes, I know," Letitia said, "and, at the time, that's what I wanted you to think. After all, when a man and a woman are thrown together on a ship like the *Splendour*, far from home with romance in the air, it's easy to believe that something might happen, especially when they spend so much time dancing in each other's arms."

"I'm not hearing anything that might change my mind," Agatha said. "When a woman like you uses her charms to snare her prey, there's generally only one outcome. Men are weak."

"Your John's not." Letitia gave a slight shake of her head. "He's not a weak man at all but he was definitely 'snared,' as you put it. Not by me, though—by you. He was constantly telling me what a wonderful dancer you were. There were even times when he tried to show me different ways to move, or different ways to transition from a step into a spin, because that was the way that you did it. He talked about you all the time. He was always nice to me, but he wasn't the least bit interested in me beyond our professional friendship. The only woman he thinks about is you. Day by day, I became so desperately jealous."

"Jealous?" Agatha could scarcely believe what she was hearing. "With the way you look . . . the hair and the eyes and . . . jealous of me?"

"Absolutely. You have to understand that John is totally and utterly in love with you. He is devoted to you and he missed you every minute of every day when we were on that ship. That's something I've never had. I've never had someone love me like that. That, most of all, is what made me jealous. I wanted what you had—what you still have—and I thought the best way to get it would be to split you up."

"That was all just an act? Your little pantomime on the ship was just to upset me?" Agatha got to her feet, seething with rage. "Get out!" she snarled. "Before I really do give you a wallop!"

"Please," Letitia said, remaining seated, "let me finish. You need to know everything."

Agatha sat down, deciding that she did, indeed, want to know the full story. After that, she'd kick Letitia out.

"Get on with it," she said. "My patience is wearing very thin."

"John went mad after you left. He was furious with me. He came to find me to make me tell you that I'd just been playacting, but by the time he did that, you'd gone. He left the ship and took a taxi to the airport, hoping to catch up with you because he thought you'd head home. Then he visited every hotel in Palma that he thought you might have checked into, but he couldn't find you."

"That's because I wasn't in Palma," Agatha said, calming herself, swirling the ice in her glass and then taking a swig. Poor John, she thought. He must have been beside himself.

"He phoned hotels all over the island," Letitia said, "but he couldn't find you anywhere. He wouldn't talk to me anymore at all, but he still wanted to do his duty and fulfil his contract until he had the chance to get back to England and find you. He even refused to dance with me when I was supposed to be helping him with demonstrations, and when the entertainments officer spoke to me about it, I had to admit that I had caused a problem. After that, basically, I had no choice but to resign."

"You lost your job?"

"It's nothing compared to the trouble I caused you. As it turns out, I'd probably have been laid off anyway. Last I heard, the *Splendour* was stranded in Lisbon with engine trouble that will take weeks to fix."

"So John's in Lisbon?"

"I doubt it. There's not much need for entertainment staff on a cruise ship with no passengers to entertain. You should call him, let him know that you know the truth. Now I . . . I think I had best go."

Agatha showed Letitia to the front door, where the dancer paused on her way out, giving Agatha a look of wide-eyed sincerity.

"I really do regret all of this," she said. "I am truly sorry."

"Well, I'm not the forgiving type," Agatha said flatly, "so don't expect any kind words from me. You did the right thing in coming here but since, by your own admission, you've never had what John and I had, you can have no idea of the damage and heartache you caused. Now bugger off. I hope I never see you again."

Chapter Ten

The night before the extravaganza, workmen laboured late into the evening. Leaving the final touches to be completed the following morning, a small convoy of cars and vans snaked out along the driveway to the main gates. Barfield House fell silent and, one by one, the lights in the windows flicked off. In Charles's study on the ground floor, the ruby glow of embers in the fireplace cast a soft, dying light over the room, barely strong enough to pick out the bulky black forms of its solid furniture.

A movement by the French doors, so slight as to be imagined, might have gone unnoticed had it not been for the muted whisper that accompanied it. Two figures crept across the room and the thin light beam from a shielded pen torch picked out a painting on the wall. Without a sound, they approached the portrait, one of them examining the frame and then swinging it out on hidden hinges. The torch beam played on the door to a wall safe where a large brass handle and two matching keyholes stood out against the dark metal. Tools were produced, the locks were picked in a matter of moments and the safe door was hauled open to reveal the inside shelves that were . . . completely bare.

The click of a wall switch suddenly flooded the room with light and the two figures froze, eyes wide with surprise behind their black masks.

"Not quite what you were expecting?" Agatha said, standing with her finger still resting on the light switch. "No expensive, sparkly, glittery things in there to tempt you?"

The two burglars dashed towards the French doors, but a uniformed police officer stepped out of the night, blocking their exit. They turned towards Agatha, but the door next to the light switch opened and Bill Wong walked in with Toni. The only other door, which led through to the drawing room, was also now standing open, with Patrick and Simon blocking the way.

A split second later, the burglars both launched themselves at the police officer, who hurled one of them to the floor in the middle of the room, the second taking the chance to duck, twist and wriggle past him. Bill sprinted across the room as the officer turned to give chase but there came a squeal and a slapping noise from outside. Charles walked in through the French doors with Gustav.

"Miss Barclay encountered a young woman on the terrace," Gustav announced, and Aurelia Barclay appeared, dragging Stuart Sculley's secretary, Yvonne, into the room by the hair, a livid red weal in the shape of a hand slap on the side of her face. Aurelia flung her captive to the floor alongside the other burglar, who pulled off his balaclava mask to reveal himself as none other than Stuart Sculley.

"I reckon she's the one who whacked me with the hammer," Aurelia said, running her fingers over the fading bruise on her jaw. "Thanks for inviting me along to see them come unstuck," she added. "Turned out to be more fun than I thought."

"You're a real live wire, aren't you, Yvonne?" Agatha said, circling the two captives slumped on the floor. "It can't have been easy keeping up with her expensive travel habits, Mr. Sculley, especially when your ex-wife had taken you for pretty much every penny you had."

"I told you this was a trap!" Yvonne hissed at Sculley.

"You should have listened to her, Mr. Sculley," Bill said. "Now you'll be going to bed in a cell instead of that nice hotel in London."

"How long did it take you to race up from London on that powerful motorbike, Stuart?" Agatha asked. "Faster than by car, I'd say. It was a clever way to establish an alibi. You drove to the hotel with the motorbike hidden in the back of your van. Then, once you'd made it look like you'd gone to bed, you sneaked down to the car park, avoiding any security cameras, then unloaded the bike. You must have also worked out where you could park the van and not be on camera—an easy thing for a security expert to do.

"Then, after you and your partner in crime had finished your latest job, you raced back down to London again. You parked the bike somewhere near the hotel—it's easy to leave the car park but it's far more hassle to drive in—and loaded it back in your van after you checked out of your room the next morning.

"You thought that, having installed the security systems in the shops you burgled, everyone would think it too ridiculous that you'd then disable your own systems to break in. In any case, you had a cast-iron alibi."

"We've got you for breaking and entering here, Mr. Sculley," Bill said. "I wonder what we'll find when we search your warehouse? In any case, now we know who we're looking for, I've no doubt forensics will be able to link you to the other crime scenes."

"DCI Wilkes is going to be so disappointed that he can't tie the burglaries in with the murder of Timothy Tinkler," Agatha said to Bill, watching the officer handcuff the prisoners.

"I'll let him know, but he's actually on leave right now," Bill said. "He should have been back, but he's stuck in Lisbon, trying to get a flight. He was supposed to be on a cruise liner, but it broke down."

Agatha gave a snort, walked over to sit in Mrs. Tassy's favourite chair, threw her head back and laughed like none of the others had ever seen her laugh before. They looked at each other in bewilderment, Charles scratched his head and Gustav fetched her a glass of brandy.

The weather for the Great Barfield Extravaganza could not have been better. A few light clouds drifted across the sky and the spring sunshine made it pleasantly warm to be out in the fresh air to enjoy all of the attractions. Charles wisely kept his welcome speech admirably short, encouraging people to sample Château Barfield from the waiters and waitresses circulating throughout the afternoon. In a marquee in one area of the lawn, there was the opportunity to enjoy a wine-tasting experience with Claudette in attendance. She had chosen a variety of good wines that would, nevertheless, show Château Barfield in a very favourable light.

Elsewhere on Barfield's huge expanse of lawn there was the chance to take a ride in a selection of steam-powered vehicles, or enjoy a whirl on the steam-powered carousel. There were a number of fairground-style attractions and a procession of vintage and classic cars whose owners took guests on short tours of the roads around the estate. Seeing the surrounding countryside from the basket of a hot-air balloon proved extremely popular, and the crowds of guests were encouraged to sample all manner of local produce from snack stands outside the house and food tables set up in the reception hall. The aerobatic display was a huge hit, there was music from brass bands, rock bands and a string quartet, the chance to ride a pony round the paddock, and dozens of businesses from across the country, including Charles's own ice-cream company, keen to show off their wares and offer samples.

Bill and Alice Wong, there by Agatha's special invitation, sought her out when they arrived slightly later than the throng of other guests, Bill having taken time to rest after the previous night's excitement.

"Alice!" Agatha greeted her friend with as close a hug

as she could manage, given the bump that lay between them. "You look fantastic!" she said, staring down at Alice's swollen stomach. Alice laughed.

"Don't look so concerned, Agatha," she said. "It's not anything you can catch from me! And once the baby's born, I've a whole exercise regime planned to get my figure back."

"How are you . . . um . . . feeling?" Agatha asked.

"Wonderful," Alice answered with a huge smile. "Apart from the nausea, the cramps, the back pain, the swollen ankles, the—"

"Enough!" Agatha said, smiling. "I don't think I've ever seen anyone look happier!"

"How about me?" Bill asked, a glass of Château Barfield now in his hand and a wide grin on his face. "Not on duty today and not driving."

"That's my job for the time being," Alice said, patting the bump.

"Well, I may have a little job for both of you later," Agatha said. "Nothing too arduous, I hope, but I know neither of you is ever really off duty."

"Always happy to help out," Bill said.

"We haven't missed the fashion show, have we?" Alice asked.

"It's just about to start and you can have a seat in the front row!" Agatha said, leading them towards the ballroom.

Guests, business owners and other contributors crowded into the ballroom for the fashion show, which was a breathtaking cavalcade of lights, colour, music and stunning fashion designs displayed by elegant models both male and female. Most of the audience found seats, and in the front row, close to Agatha and Alice, sat Mrs. Tassy, dressed not in her customary black but in a wispy ensemble of red-and-blue chiffon which, in Agatha's opinion, made her look twenty-five years younger.

With the fashion show over, darkness was beginning to fall outside, and Martin Randall appeared on the catwalk to announce that, while the stage was dismantled to prepare for the charity auction, those who were interested could preview the catalogue items where they were displayed in the drawing room. For everyone else, further refreshments would be served on the terrace from where a fireworks display could be viewed shortly.

Agatha stood on the terrace with Charles, watching people drifting into the drawing room. Her clock was displayed on a table in the far corner of the room, near the fireplace.

"I think it's all gone tremendously well," Charles said. "A huge success! Thank you, Aggie!"

Agatha looked at him, about to chastise him for the "Aggie," when a tall man with a slim, dark-haired woman on his arm went into the drawing room.

"Who's that?" she asked.

"That's old Binkie," Charles replied. "You know him. You met when we—"

"Not him. The woman."

"His latest squeeze," Charles said, waggling his eyebrows. "Don't know her name. She's new. Apparently, he only met her a few days ago."

Agatha took her phone from her bag and sent a two-word group message: *She's here.* Her whole team was now on the alert. She watched from the terrace while guests shuffled around the drawing room, examining the items bearing auction lot numbers. When the first of the fireworks went off, the drawing room emptied, everyone hurrying outside to watch the display. Only Binkie's "latest squeeze" stayed behind. Agatha shrank back against the wall, urging Charles to do likewise. Having previously ignored the clock, the woman now walked straight up to it, opened the face and set the hands to twelve o'clock.

A fusillade of fireworks drowned out the delicate tones of the "Wiener Carneval" and when the dancers twirled to their full height, the woman gently pulled out the minute hand and counted out the one-two-three combination. She then stood back to watch the enamel panel illustrations all slowly slide forward, revealing themselves as drawers lined with soft, green felt. The woman stared at the drawers, her fists clenched.

"Looking for these?" Agatha walked into the room with Charles at her shoulder, the fireworks outside thundering colour across the sky. In her outstretched hand she showed a selection of gemstones that changed from a deep purple-red colour to an emerald green as she passed beneath the dazzling chandelier that hung from the ceiling.

"I don't know what . . ." the woman said, hesitantly, in a lightly accented voice.

"Oh, I think you do, Hedwig . . . or is it Hedy . . . no, it's neither, of course, but let's make it Hedy. Dark hair suits you better than the blonde wig you wore at the auction house."

Bill came into the room from the library with Alice and

Gustav. Mrs. Tassy, desperate not to miss this show-down, walked in off the terrace with Claudette, Toni and Simon. The door to the corridor opened and Patrick entered, accompanied by Tristan.

"You!" the woman gasped. "But you're dead!"

"I've been getting that a lot recently," Tristan said, glowering at her.

"I have no idea what this is about!" the woman squawked.

"Yes, you do, Hedy," Agatha said, holding the hand-ful of stones just out of the woman's reach. "It's about these—alexandrite. My clock's history is hazy but there was thought to be a Russian connection. That's where the stones came from. These were mined in Russia's Ural Mountains. I'm told that the quality of these stones is unmatched. My gem expert had never seen anything like them. They may be worth up to ten times more than diamonds and these are only a few of the stones that were in the secret drawers."

"I just thought the clock looked interesting!" the woman defended herself.

"That's crap, Hedy! You know all about the clock! You know the dancers rise to release the drawers and you know the combination to unlock them. You expected to find the drawers full of alexandrite. Sadly for you, you're not the only thief to have found the cupboard bare at Barfield of late."

"You're wrong, I . . ." The woman took a step towards the hall door, and Tristan stepped forward to face her.

"We're not wrong! It was you that made the big mis-take!" he roared above a clamour of fireworks. "You sent two men to get the clock and told them to get my brother to tell them where it was at all costs. You sent the men who murdered my brother!"

Patrick drew Tristan away from the woman.

"Brother . . ." the woman said, realising who Tristan was.

"Everyone in this room," Agatha said, closing her fingers around the stones and waving her arm around the room, "was a friend of the man you had killed. We're sort of like a distant, extended family. I'm guessing that was one of your problems, wasn't it? Family.

"The clock must have been passed down through generations of your family in Austria, if that's where you come from, and then sold by someone who had no idea what was hidden in it. Those who did know, however, wanted it back. You were one of those who knew its true value."

"Why did you stop bidding and walk out of the auction?" asked Martin Randall, who had been listening from outside, wary of what might be happening to his auction lots.

"Because the price was about to get silly," Agatha answered when the woman responded with nothing more than a pout. "She found the clock almost by accident, up for sale in a small country auction house. If she'd carried on matching my bids, the price might have gone so high that people would be talking about it. You would be boasting about it on your website, Martin. The press might even take an interest. If all that happened, others in her family would get to hear about it, and they would come after her for their share."

"You know nothing about this clock!" the woman

screamed. "The clock is rightly mine! It should have been passed to me. Those stones are mine, not yours!"

"You're wrong about that," Randall said. "Agatha bought the clock perfectly legally. The clock and anything in it belong to her."

"You couldn't accept that, though, could you, Hedy?" Agatha said. "So you hired two thugs off the street to steal it for you, and that all went very badly. Timothy Tinkler was killed. Then you got them to try kidnapping me, and they even torched my make-up . . . I mean . . . my car. You're going to jail."

"I don't know the men you are talking about. You can't prove any of that!" the woman hissed, stomping towards Bill and Alice. "Now get out of my way. I am leaving!"

Bill and Alice stood their ground and then, during a moment's lull in the fireworks, a phone pinged in the woman's pocket.

"Don't you want to see who the message is from, Hedy?" Agatha asked. "No, wait a minute, there's no need," she added, holding up the phone now in her hand. "It's from me, using the phone you gave to the thugs who killed Timothy Tinkler. They will identify you, and this proves you were in contact with them."

"Where did you get that?" the woman demanded.

"There was an attempted robbery at Mr. Tinkler's antiques shop the other night," Agatha said, stretching the truth slightly. "One of your two thugs left this behind. The only things on it are messages passed between you and them."

The climax of the fireworks display came with a mighty explosion that rattled the glass of the French doors.

"Oh, dear, Hedy," Agatha said sadly. "I think that was all your hopes and dreams going up in smoke . . ."

Alice, still a serving police officer who, unlike her husband, had not consumed any alcohol, advised the woman that she was being arrested on suspicion of being an accessory to murder, then explained her rights while Bill called Mircester Police Station.

"Come on, Martin," Agatha said. "You still have an auction to run, and that clock is still up for grabs. The bidders will be waiting."

"And the alexandrite?" asked Randall.

"That's mine," Agatha replied. "There will be special bonuses for my staff, who've all worked their socks off, and something by way of compensation for Tristan, but, as you said, I bought the clock fair and square along with whatever was in it. Now let's get that auction underway before we're all dragged off to make statements!"

"Well, I must say, old girl, I didn't think we'd be back here again quite so soon." Charles seated Agatha at a table in the Ebrington Arms, the dust having settled on the huge success of the Great Barfield Extravaganza long enough for them to enjoy a celebratory visit to the pub where they had started it all.

Agatha paused, irked by the "old girl" remark, but then chose to ignore it. It was a struggle, but she refused to let her temper throw her plans for the rest of the day off course. He took his seat opposite her.

"We're almost becoming regulars!" He laughed and

228

she smiled. "You know, there was a time, not so long ago, when we had quite a few little regular haunts. An afternoon jaunt to a country inn would turn into an evening meal after a couple of bottles of wine and then we would . . ."

"I know, Charles. One of the things that makes me a good detective is that I have a very good memory." She picked up the menu, browsed through the temptations on offer and then set it aside.

"I'm guessing you're going to say that what we had is all in the past," he said, a look of forlorn resignation flitting across his features. "I'm guessing you're going to say that you don't want to talk about the past, but I miss all that ever so much, you know, Aggie."

There was that name again. It rankled even more than "old girl" but she took a deep breath, maintained her composure and kept her thoughts on track.

"Actually, I *do* want to talk about the past," she said. "I've been thinking quite a lot about the past recently and I've come to some intriguing conclusions. I'd be interested to know what you think."

The waitress arrived and Agatha finally decided against having lunch but, with Charles's enthusiastic agreement, ordered a bottle of the primitivo they had enjoyed on their previous visit.

"I'm more than happy to listen," Charles said as the waitress departed, "if you want to reminisce about the good old days."

"It's not *our* past I want to talk about," Agatha replied. "It's *the* past. Events around here in the distant past—the 1660s."

"Aha!" Charles grinned. "The Campden Wonder. I knew that would tickle your fancy!"

"Yes," Agatha agreed, then asked the waitress, who had returned with the wine, just to pour rather than going through the pantomime of tasting. "You thought a mystery that had gone unsolved for more than three hundred and sixty years would exercise my little grey cells, as Hercule Poirot would say."

Agatha took a sip of wine, her eyes never leaving Charles. He shifted uncomfortably but maintained a boyish smile that, at one time, might have charmed her.

"To tell you the truth, with everything else that's been going on, William Harrison's story turned into a real distraction," she continued, "but I couldn't help delving into it from time to time. I'm sure you already know that there's been quite a lot written about it over the years.

"Harrison's own tale of having been wounded by his kidnappers, then taken on horseback to the east of England before being bundled aboard a ship days later seems fairly unlikely to me. Somewhere along the way he would have been able to leave word with someone at an inn or at the port, to let his family know what was happening to him. That kidnap scenario seems pretty dubious. Neither do I think, as some people do, that Harrison was kidnapped and passed from one gang to another, or sold on, with each purchaser hoping to make a profit from either a ransom or a reward."

"There was a thriving trade at the time whereby people were kidnapped in Britain and shipped across the Atlantic," Charles pointed out. "They were forced to work as indentured servants or labourers."

"Those were mainly young people and children, Charles," Agatha argued, "not old men like Harrison. Workers were a valuable commodity but an old man wouldn't be seen as such—more of a liability, really. Who'd want to pay for a servant who might snuff it after a couple of years? No, if Harrison was kidnapped at all, I believe it would have been for ransom, since he was a trusted employee of a wealthy family, or perhaps for more sinister reasons."

"Ah, the skulduggery theories!" Charles grinned.

"Apparently, there were lots of strange things going on in England in those days," Agatha went on, enjoying her wine as she picked up the tale. "There were lots of clandestine political deals being struck and plenty of secrets being kept under wraps by the upper classes. Ordinary people suffered most from all the death and destruction during the Civil War, as ordinary people always do. I should think most of them just wanted to get on with their lives in peace, but the aristocrats and wealthy merchants who had lost power, grand houses and vast estates were different. Those who had lost property, status and influence wanted it all back—and they'd stop at nothing to get it."

"You've really been doing your research, haven't you?" Charles sounded impressed.

"Oh, come on, Sir Charles Fraith of Barfield House— you know exactly what I'm talking about. You'd do anything to keep your family seat, including dodgy

business deals, grabbing at outrageously shady invest-
ment opportunities and even marrying completely the
wrong woman! I've hauled your arse out of that mess
more than once . . ."

"I say, I think that's a little—"

"Oh, shut up, Charles!" Agatha snapped, then took a
sip of wine while glancing at her watch. "I've a lot to get
through and I don't want you throwing me off course.
Because of all the 'skulduggery,' as you put it, any number of theories have been proposed about how William
Harrison might have been abducted due to him, through
his position with the Noel family, knowing too many
secrets. Maybe somebody wanted him out of the way
until whatever underhand deal they were negotiating
could be signed and sealed without the danger of him
scuppering it.

"It's even been suggested that Harrison was sent on
some kind of secret mission by Lady Juliana Noel—
something to do with land and politics that kept him
away for all those months. Like Harrison's own story
about ending up in Turkey, escaping and having to find
his way all the way home to Chipping Campden, I think
that's total bollocks."

"If his story isn't true," Charles said, watching Agatha top up her glass, "then why would he lie? Harrison
was known to be an honest, reliable, trustworthy man."

"Exactly!" Agatha said, swallowing some wine and
giving Charles a sideways look. "If he wasn't whisked
off in a ship somewhere, where did he go? What is his
secret? What are the secrets that men like to keep? In
my experience, it all comes down to money and sex. So

could it have been money? Had the respectable, highly regarded William Harrison run up massive debts, perhaps through gambling? Did he run off with the rents he collected in order to pay off his debts and then stay out of the way long enough to give his kidnap story some credence? I doubt it, simply because he really was such a fine, upstanding pillar of the community, and utterly loyal to the Noel family. He wouldn't steal from them.

"In any case, I've read that there was far more money in Harrison's house than he had in his possession when he went missing. If he really needed money, why not just stage a robbery like the one that had happened a few months previously?"

"Perhaps that break-in *was* actually staged," Charles suggested. "Harrison could have had money problems going back a long way."

"I considered that, but it seems unlikely," Agatha replied. "Again, it doesn't fit with Harrison's character—his highly respectable image and his allegiance to the Noels. So was it sex? Had he sloped off for a few months to spend some time with a secret mistress until the money he'd collected that day ran out? I don't believe that, for all the reasons I've just mentioned. If Harrison suddenly decided to have a final fling with a mistress, then there was far more money available to him that he could have used to prolong the affair.

"No, the idea that Harrison ran off with a mistress for a while just doesn't make sense. Neither, of course, do poor John Perry's rambling accusations, confessions, denials and, ultimately, his silence when his whole family went to the gallows."

"That, indeed, is the crux of the matter," Charles said, nodding.

"So, if William Harrison wasn't abducted, where the hell did he go?" She took another sip of wine and he sat back in his chair, arms folded, waiting for her theory to unfold. "Actually, I don't think he went anywhere at all—well, certainly not very far. You see, despite the fact that William Harrison didn't die, I think that the Campden Wonder is still very much a murder story. Consider this . . ." Agatha sat forward in her chair, Charles half expecting she was about to stand up and pace the room, as though playing the part of a barrister in a courtroom drama. "We know that William Harrison was a proud man, devoted to the Noel family. He expected to work for Lady Juliana until the day he died and that his son would then take over from him. When his house was broken into and money stolen, that money was undoubtedly in his care prior to being passed on to her ladyship. He must have been devastated that such a thing had happened. He would have been distraught at the thought of having let Lady Juliana down. His house was secure and the money had been well hidden. How did the thieves know the best way to break in, and where to find the cash? If it were me, I'd suspect an inside job."

"John Perry, of course, later confirmed that to be the case."

"He did," Agatha agreed, "and, despite the fact that John was at church with the Harrisons when the break-in happened, William Harrison must immediately have suspected him of having colluded with his family in the burglary. Harrison would have known pretty much

234

everyone in the area, and he would have known that John's brother, Richard, and mother, Joan, were not well respected. In fact, they were regarded as local lowlifes. People around Chipping Campden took such a dim view of the family that some even believed Joan Perry was a witch. I think that John Perry was a simple soul who had been employed by William Harrison almost as an act of charity—maybe even to get him away from the bad influence of his mother and brother."

"That would fit with William Harrison's image of being a fine, upstanding, compassionate sort of chap," commented Charles.

"Perhaps," Agatha said, enjoying a little more wine. "But John Perry was also someone who would do what he was told. He was vulnerable, easily led and easily confused. I think Harrison knew that he had been burgled by Richard and Joan Perry long before John confessed it to the magistrate. I doubt it would have been difficult for Harrison to bully or frighten John into telling him the truth about the burglary. That's when he came up with the idea to stage his own death. Ultimately, he turned the fiction into a kidnap scenario."

"You think Harrison faked his abduction?"

"Almost certainly. John Perry will have helped him, having had the fear of God put into him by Harrison, who may even have used the nonsense about Joan being a witch to get John to do and say whatever he wanted him to. Harrison planted his hat and bloodstained scarf for searchers to find and then made himself scarce, hiding out not too far away—possibly even in his own house with the connivance of his wife and son.

"When John Perry was first held in jail, it seems that pretty much anyone had access to him. They brought him ale, everyone keen to be the one who solicited the truth from him about what had happened to his master. Harrison may well have been feeding Perry outlandish tales to tell. I'm pretty sure his son, Edward, will have played a part in that. Then, when the time came, Perry was instructed to accuse his mother and brother of Harrison's murder."

"Do you really think John would do something like that at the bidding of William Harrison?" Charles asked. "Even if he wasn't very bright, he would have known that they would be sent to the gallows."

"I believe that Harrison persuaded John that it was all a ploy to get them to confess to the burglary," Agatha explained. "I think that he, or his son, or maybe even his wife, were the ones who told John how he should keep changing his story and that they also made sure the Perrys knew about the Indemnity and Oblivion Act, resulting in them admitting to the burglary.

"John will have been told that, once this happened, his brother and mother would be kept in jail for a while—that would serve as their punishment—but that William Harrison would then reappear long before they ever faced the hangman's noose. He didn't, of course, but Edward was reported to be there at the gallows steps, perhaps reassuring John that William would be along any moment."

"So you think that William Harrison left the Perry family to die?" Charles asked. "Why did he have to let that happen?"

"He didn't," Agatha said. "But, while William Harrison was not a murder victim, he was most certainly a murderer. He didn't *have* to let them die, he *chose* to do so. He knew they would all hang and he planned it that way all along. He murdered them as surely as if he had shot them all dead. He had a classic motive—revenge. As far as he was concerned, the Perrys had made him look incompetent and had endangered his livelihood, as well as that of his son. His pride had been compromised and he felt they had damaged his trustworthy reputation in the eyes of the Noel family. Their money had been stolen while it was in his care, after all. Satisfying his revenge by showing up at the Perrys' home with a couple of well-armed heavies was an option, but beating the crap out of them risked leaving a stain on his character that might affect his status in the community. Instead, he followed the lead of the upper classes and indulged in a little skulduggery, keeping his hands clean but condemning the Perrys to death."

"What happened to the money?" asked Charles. "If the Perrys really did steal it, they couldn't have spent it all. Once they confessed, wouldn't they have to return it?"

"Why would they agree to do that? They expected to be set free after the robbery trial. They knew they hadn't murdered William Harrison, after all, and John may even have assured them the old man was set to show up and clear them of the murder charge. They might have been counting on using the money to leave the area once they got out of jail. Wherever they hid it, or buried it, my guess is it's still there.

"That, then, is my take on the Campden Wonder." Agatha drained her glass. "William Harrison used the judicial system to murder all three Perrys in revenge for them having robbed and humiliated him."

Placing her glass on the table, she caught a glimpse of her lipstick stains on the rim. She would have to re-apply, almost excusing herself in order to head for the ladies,' then checking her watch again and deciding against it. Charles should see her making sure that she looked her best. She took her lipstick and a compact mirror from her handbag, then made a show of repainting her lips.

"I think you've come up with an excellent theory," Charles said, finishing his own glass and holding up the empty bottle. "Why don't we order another of these? It's far too late for lunch now, but we can easily while away the rest of the afternoon, think about an early dinner, then perhaps leave the car here and take a taxi back to—"

"I'm afraid I have other plans, *old boy*," Agatha said, standing and looking towards the door. John Glass had just walked in. "I don't need a taxi. My handsome driver has arrived. We're off to a tea dance in Worcester, followed by dinner at the Feathers in Ancombe. I'd suggest you join us but you don't have a partner and, well, you've never really been much of a dancer anyway, have you?"

With her coat and handbag over one arm, she tweaked his cheek with her free hand, then left him sitting on his own as she strode over to John. She put her arms around him and kissed him on the lips with such passion that it brought a cheer from two real-ale drinkers standing at the bar. Agatha looked over at them and winked.

"That was the best welcome I've ever had," John said, catching his breath and smiling. "Not that I'm complaining, but what happened to your 'no public displays of affection' rule?"

"It's a rule that's there to be broken," Agatha said. "Spend too much time worrying about rules and you'll have no time left to live your life. Now," she added, linking her arm through his, "take me dancing so that I can work up an appetite for dinner and for . . . whatever else takes our fancy."

Charles watched them leave and called for the bill. Things had not gone entirely as he had expected with Agatha, but when had they ever? She was a formidable woman with a stubbornly independent streak, determined to enjoy life to the full. How was it, then, that she could choose to be with her dancing retired policeman instead of enjoying all he could offer—the estate, the grand house and the burgeoning new businesses? Gazing out through the window, he saw John's car leaving the car park. He shook his head in resignation at the thought of her, the great detective and hard-nosed businesswoman, heading off to a genteel tea dance. He smiled. For now, she was gone, and he had no choice but to bide his time, gather his thoughts and come up with a new tactic. He had lost this battle, but not the whole war. Agatha Raisin, after all, was worth fighting for.

About the Author

Louise Bowles

M. C. Beaton, hailed as the "Queen of Crime" by *The Globe and Mail,* was the author of the *New York Times* and *USA Today* bestselling Agatha Raisin novels—the basis for the hit series on Acorn TV and public television—as well as the Hamish Macbeth series and the Edwardian Murder Mysteries featuring Lady Rose Summer. Born in Scotland, she started her career writing historical romances under several pseudonyms and her maiden name, Marion Chesney. Her books have sold more than twenty-four million copies worldwide.

A longtime friend of M. C. Beaton's, **R.W. Green** has written numerous works of fiction and nonfiction. He lives in Surrey with his family and a black Labrador called Flynn.